Christy Miller's Diary

*Christy Miller's Diary*

Published in association with the Books & Such Literary Agency, Janet Kobobel Grant, 52 Mission Circle, Suite 122, PMB 170, Santa Rosa, CA 95409-5370, www.booksandsuch.biz.

Published by      Robin's Nest Productions, Inc.
P.O. BOX 56353
Portland, OR 97238

Printed in the United States of America by BelieversPress, Bloomington, Minnesota 55438

# Christy Miller's Diary

## ROBIN JONES GUNN

Robin's Nest Productions

Portland, Oregon

## September 2

My Uncle Bob gave me this diary today. He told me to try to write in it every day and write about what I'm feeling and thinking. He said this little book might become a real friend to me. I think he knew I could really use a friend right now. This move to California and starting my sophomore year at a new school and everything is pretty scary.

So, dear diary—dear new friend—hello. What should I call you? You can call me Christy. Or Chris. Actually, only a few people call me Chris. I like Christy better. Or you can call me by my full name—Christina Juliet Miller

Actually, you aren't going to be calling me anything, are you? You're my silent friend. My Dear Silent Friend. DSF. That's what I'll call you.

DSF
Dear Silent Friend,

This is the beginning of what I hope will be a long and happy friendship, DSF.

September 3

Well, DSF,

I should tell you about Alissa. I met her earlier this summer when I was visiting my aunt and uncle here in California. I thought I wanted to be just like Alissa and then I found out that she had a lot of difficult stuff in her life. She actually told me she thought I had it good because I had a "normal" family and was still innocent.

I got a letter from her yesterday. Alissa said she didn't understand what I meant when I wrote and told her that I'd given my heart to Jesus. She said why would I give my heart to someone who is dead and why would I make promises to a man who no longer exists. I know she said that because of Shawn. When Shawn died a few months ago she acted as if it didn't matter to her at all. But I know it did. It had to.

I don't know how to tell her what I believe and why I gave my heart to Christ. Maybe I can try to explain it to you and if it sounds right, I'll write the same thing to her.

The only way I can explain it is that it's as if there's this secret place in my heart and before, I'd go there and it always felt lonely. It was quiet. Too quiet. I could go there and be alone to think but it was always so empty. When I surrendered my life to the Lord, it was as if He came into that secret place and now He's there. I know He's there. He listens. He knows. He understands.

How do I explain that to someone else? Especially to Alissa who has so much hurt in her heart. I imagine the secret place in her heart must be all closed up and locked tight. I wonder if she even goes there anymore.

## September 4

DSF - Hi.

Me again. Well, I have big news, DSF. We went to Escondido today and looked at the house we're going to move into and I think I've found my first friend. Her name is Brittany. She reminds me of Alissa in some ways. Intriguing and intimidating at the same time. She's the kind of girl I always think I want to be like, but when I'm around her, I feel as though I'm not on the same level. I think I'd like to be like her, because Brittany seems so mature and experienced. Not clumsy, the way I am.

Still, I don't know. I liked having Paula for my best friend because we seemed to be the same in so many ways. At least we used to be. I think I'd like to be more sophisticated, like Brittany.

Things feel a lot different here than how it was in Wisconsin. Paula and I were close friends ever since we were little.

But this summer Paula found a new best friend and I think that even if my family hadn't moved here, Paula and I still wouldn't be the closest of friends back at Brightwater High School this year.

## September 12

So much has been happening, DSF!

I haven't been able to write everything down because it seems like there's not enough time. The thing I've been thinking about is Rick, this guy that I met in the craziest way. I went to a sleep over at Janelle's and we went out T.P.ing and when we were putting the toilet paper all over Rick's house, he came out and I was hiding in the bushes and I started running, and… oh, I don't even want to talk about it. It was definitely the most embarrassing moment of my life ever.

The thing is, now Brittany says Rick has been asking about me at school. He's real tall and good looking. Everybody knows him. He's on the football team. I can't imagine a guy like Rick being interested in me.

What do you think?

## September 14

Dear Silent Friend of Mine,

I haven't told you about Todd yet, have I? I thought of that a couple days ago after I told you about Rick. Todd is my idea of the perfect guy. I met him this summer on the beach. It was the same day I met Alissa and some other people. I think if I had you to confide in during the summer I would have filled all your pages just talking about Todd, my summer surfer dream boy. He's not like any other guy I've ever known. You should see his screaming silver blue eyes! And his smile! Oh!

Can you keep a secret? Yes, I guess you can. Todd kissed me on July 28 and gave me a bouquet of white carnations. It was the most romantic moment of my life. I still have the carnations. They're all dried out. I stuck them in a coffee can when we moved here.

However, there's one slightly huge problem with Todd. He's in Florida now, at his mom's. He said he'd write me but he never did. I'll probably never see him again. I think the rest of my life I'll always have sweet memories of Todd, even if we never see each other again.

*September 20*

Hi, DSF.

I've been thinking about Alissa's questions some more, from her letter. She asked why I'd make promises to someone who is dead and I know now that I can tell her that Jesus isn't dead. He rose from the dead and He's alive. That's what makes Christianity different from all other religions. That what makes it real.

I found this verse last night when I was looking in the back of my Bible for verses about the heart. It's long, but here's the whole verse, or actually three verses.

"For I know the plans I have for you," declares the Lord, "plans to prosper you and not to harm you, plans to give you hope and a future. Then you will call upon me and come and pray to me, and I will listen to you. You will seek me and find me when you seek me with all your heart" Jeremiah 29:11.

I like that so much because she asked why I'd make promises to a man who no longer exists. The thing is, He does exist! I made only one promise to Him—to turn over my whole life and my whole heart to Him alone. And He made all these promises to me!

    - to prosper me and not to harm me
    - give me hope and a future

- listen to me
- that I'd find Him when I seek Him with all my heart

Okay. Now I have to go write this to Alissa before I forget it all. Bye!

## September 28

I just read that last entry, DSF.

I feel bad because I never did get around to writing to Alissa. But I've been learning some new things.

Here are a few key words for you to hold on to for me. Katie Christian and Peter Pagan. At Sunday School a few days ago they talked about missionary dating when you try to bring the other person up to where you're at with the Lord. It's always easier for them to bring you down. I don't think I'll need to remember that for my own life, but I want to remember the thought.

My dad got really mad because I didn't tell them I was going out to pizza with Katie and Rick after church. He told me I was using up my youth too fast and once it was gone I wouldn't be able to get it back.

The thing is, I'm not really trying to grow up too fast. All these things are happening to me, and I'm just trying to keep up with them. I think it would be different if I were rebelling or something. But I'm trying to do the right thing. Well, at least most of the time.

I'm sure Dad's right, that I don't always think things through. But he doesn't know all the good choices I've made or all the stuff I've already said no to.

I've been trying to figure out what God wants me to do. I think He wants me to try really hard to do the right thing and say no to everything that looks like it wouldn't be good for me.

No, no, no, no. There, my daily practice in saying no.

## October 5

Two days, DSF!

Two days until I go to Palm Springs with Janelle and Brittany! Yipeeeeee! My Uncle Bob is going to a golf tournament in Palm Springs and so my aunt invited me to come with her and bring some friends. I wanted Katie to go with me. She's my new friend from school. I met her at Janelle's party. Katie has the prettiest red hair. It's very distinctive and so is she. Katie is our school mascot—the Kelley High Cougar. So she can't go because of the football game on Friday night.

Janelle and Brittany are coming with me instead. I know I'm going to have a great time with both of them. They are really popular and I think we're getting to be pretty good friends.

My little brother fell off his bike yesterday. We had to rush him to the emergency room because he was bleeding so bad and it wouldn't stop. He ended up with four stitches and you'd think it was forty the way he howled when the doctor started working on him! Dad told me I need to help out more around the house because Mom's going to be working now. Then David begged me to wait on him because he said his chin hurt too much for him to get off the couch to get himself something to drink. Oh, brother!

Only two more days of being everyone's slave and then I get to go to Palm Springs! I can't wait! We are going to have so much fun!

## October 10

Oh, man, oh, man, my DSF!

What a nightmare I've just gone through. The trip to Palm Springs with Aunt Marti and my friends turned into a disaster. Brittany has so many problems. She lied to me a bunch of times and tried to bring me down with her. I can't believe I didn't see it coming. Am I too trusting of people or what?

I still can't believe what happened. Brittany got Janelle and me in trouble with the police when she shoplifted and also stole prescription diet pills. And then she and Janelle both ran from the security guard and left me alone! I can't believe I'm even writing this down. It was the worst thing I have ever gone through in my life. We had to come home early and everything was ruined.

Tracy sent me a note before we went to Palm Springs. She wrote out a verse that really helped me when we went through that whole thing with the police and the questioning. I promised myself I'd look the verse up in my Bible and underline it. I also want to write it here so you can remind me, DSF, when I read this again someday, how much that verse meant to me when I needed it most. Here it is:

"The Lord himself goes before you and will be with you; he will never leave you nor forsake you. Do not be afraid; do not be discouraged" Deuteronomy 31:8.

My dad put me on restriction. Two weeks of no social activities. The only thing that's going to be hard is not going to church and seeing Rick. I never see him at school. That afternoon at Pizza Hut was the best time I've had since we moved here. Rick's probably already forgotten about it. He'll probably have another girlfriend by the time I get off restriction.

Why do guys do that? They act interested in you, and then they forget about you.

Like Todd. I'll never forget Todd. Ever. But I bet if he saw me right now he wouldn't even remember my name. If only guys weren't so weird. If only they…

## October 11

Sorry I stopped in the middle of a sentence last time yesterday, DSF.

I was dropping off into the land of 'If Only' and with all that had gone wrong in my life, I knew that I'd end up getting depressed and staying very depressed thinking about Todd and Rick. And then guess what happened today? Rick asked me to homecoming. No, of course I'm not going. My parents are really strict about dating. But you know what he said? He said the most beautiful girls are the innocent ones. And that my honesty intrigued him. He also said for a girl like me, he could wait until I was old enough to be allowed to go out with him. That means my 16th birthday next July 27th. He was so sweet and understanding. He said he'd see me at church on Sunday and that he'd call me sometime. I'm so glad I'm not on phone restriction along with everything else!

And THEN, as if that wasn't enough to make my day, I came home, the phone rang, David said it was a guy and so of course, I thought it was Rick. I picked up the phone and said, 'Hi, Rick' and it wasn't Rick!!!

It was TODD!!!!

He was calling me from his mom's in Florida. I had almost given up on ever hearing from him. It's been over three months. His voice sounded soooooo good! We talked a really long time. I told him all about Palm Springs and he told me this long story about letting go of things that I didn't need to hold onto anymore. That was what I've been trying to do by learning how to say 'no' all the time. But then Todd said it wasn't enough to just say no. I needed to start saying 'yes' to the right stuff. I especially need to start saying 'yes' to God. It was SOOOOO cool.

And the best news of all is that Todd is moving back to California. He's going to be here by Christmas! I can't wait to see him again!!

This has been such a perfect day! After everything turned into such a disaster last weekend, it's as if God is turning everything around for good.

I'm so happy right now. I really, honestly feel peace in that secret place in my heart. I haven't felt this close to God since last summer on the beach with Todd and his friends, Doug and Tracy, and all the other Christians I met. I wish we could all get together and sit around the campfire pit on the beach and sing again. Todd said that when he comes at Christmas he wants us to have breakfast on the beach. That is going to be so AWESOME (to use Doug's word)!! Todd told me to start practicing making scrambled eggs.

Well, I better go. I did finally write Alissa and I told her that Jesus wasn't dead. He's very much alive! And very present in my life. I forgot to tell her all the other stuff from that verse about the plans God has for us. Maybe God had me find that verse just for me because it is really true in my life right now. I know God has a plan to give me hope and a future. All I pray is that I will keep seeking Him with all my heart.

You keep reminding me of that, okay, DSF? I'm counting on you to hold these words for me so I can come back and read them again when I need to be reminded. Okay? Thank you, my Dear Silent Friend. What would I do without you?

## November 27

Dear Friend Who Happens to be Silent,

I wish you could speak up now. I need some advice. I'm starting to buy Christmas presents and I don't know what to do. Should I buy something for Todd? I'm pretty sure I'm going to get something for Rick. But what should I get them? And is it strange to be giving gifts to two different guys? Well? Speak up!

## December 21

Dear Silent Friend,

Now I'm glad you can't speak. I need you to hold another secret for me. I saw Rick tonight and do you know what happened? He kissed me. It was quick and sort of pushy, if you know what I mean. I didn't expect it at all.

17

Then I gave him the CD I bought him and he kissed me again. The second kiss was longer and I knew he was going to do it. And you know what I did? I pulled away and then it got all awkward and he said we should go back in the church gym. But it was like he was mad at me.

The worst part was that afterwards he totally ignored me. I don't know what I should have done differently. I feel so mixed up right now. I've thought about kisses before, you know. I think that's normal—to wonder what it would be like to be kissed. But I never thought seriously about kissing Rick or what it would be like for him to kiss me. And I guess I wasn't ready. Maybe I should think this through some more before I see Rick again... that is, if he's still speaking to me.

## December 22

Okay, DSF,

Now all I can think about is kisses and kissing. I'm going to see Todd in a few days. What if he kisses me again like he did last summer? How many kisses do I want to give away? I've never thought this through before. I think kisses should mean something very special and should be given away very sparingly while I'm young. I'm 15, you know. Does that seem young to you? It does to me. At least it does today.

## December 25

Christmas Day
Well, DSF,

After all these long weeks of waiting, I finally saw Todd this morning. We had breakfast on the beach, as he promised. And now I'm perplexed.

It seems that when dreams come true, they never turn out the same way you dreamed them. They twist and turn and disappoint, leaving you wanting so much more. I don't know which to blame: The dream itself or the reality that dissolves the dream.

Surely there has never been a more non-committal guy on the face of the earth than Todd Spencer. He spent more time skim boarding on the beach with David this morning than he spent with me. And then he took off right after we were done eating, or should I say, done eating what the sea gulls left for us! He said he was going to Shawn's parents' house since this is the first Christmas since Shawn died. I know that was a good thing for him to do and a good reason for him to leave, but I can barely describe to you how I felt as I sat alone by the dwindling fire, watching Todd walk away. He was supposed to have his arms around me. Instead, his arms were full of camping gear.

He didn't even look back.

This was our dream breakfast and it was over almost before it began. I'd have to say the best word to describe what I felt is abandoned. I felt forsaken. I know God will never abandon me or forsake me. I guess friends do sometimes. Even special friends. Even Todd.

All I can say is that this week, I've got to find out where I stand with Todd. I need to know where our relationship is and where it's going. This is too important to me to just let it go slipping away.

## December 27

You aren't going to be very proud of me, my Dear Silent Friend,

I played some pointless games today with my friends. The thing is, at the time, it didn't seem like they were games or that I was doing anything I'd regret later. But now I feel awful. I wish I had this day to live over again.

You see, we all went ice skating. And Heather told me I should try to make Todd jealous by skating with Doug. Then Doug asked me to skate and we were pretty good. And it was fun. But you should have seen the way Todd looked at us.

Then we went to eat and Todd kept giving me these puppy dog looks as if he wanted me to go sit next to him or maybe he just wanted me to see how left out he felt. I know that feeling. I've felt that way lots of times. I felt that way last summer when Todd took me to a concert. I thought it was just going to be the two of us and then it ended up being a whole bunch of people who were already friends and I felt so left out.

It didn't get much better after we left the restaurant. Doug gave me his jacket before we went into the restaurant because I was so cold and then Tracy was saying how cold she was when we left, so I gave his jacket to her and she gave me the strangest look. Then I figured it out. She didn't want Doug's jacket. She wanted Doug to put his arm around her!

Tracy likes Doug!!!!!

I didn't see it before but it makes sense now. When she and I were making cookies the other day she said she was going to give some to a guy she liked but she wouldn't tell me who he was. Now I know. It was Doug! And I spent the whole day skating and everything with Doug and she must have been so jealous.

I have a headache thinking about all this. How am I going to patch things up so we can all be friends again? I'm only staying here at the beach at my aunt and uncle's house for the rest of this week and then I go back home to Escondido. And I'm not looking forward to going to school after Christmas vacation and running into Rick.

Why does life have to be so complicated?

*December 28*

I'm back, DSF.

And as if that last entry wasn't enough to keep me tossing and turning all night, guess who sent me a letter here at my aunt and uncle's house?

Alissa.

She said she lost my address in Escondido. And that's not all she said. She told me she's pregnant. My hand is shaking as I write this. She's pregnant. I still can't believe it. I started crying so hard when I read her letter. She asked me to pray for her and I did. A lot. I fell asleep for awhile and now it's the middle of the night and very quiet. I think I woke up because there's so much on my mind. My body fell asleep, but my mind didn't. It kept going and going until all my wild dreams woke me up.

The only good thing I can think of right now is that Alissa said she thought about having an abortion, but then changed her mind because a friend of hers had one a few years ago and then wished she hadn't. Alissa said she'd probably have the baby and then put it up for adoption. I pray that's what she does. Alissa also said she went to a Crisis Pregnancy Center and the counselor there gave her a Bible. I pray she reads that Bible until the words break through into that secret place in her heart. God's words are like rays of light. They can slip through the tiniest opening and make all the darkness instantly disappear.

I know that's true for Alissa but it's also true for me and my problems with my friends. Although my problems seem like nothing compared to what Alissa is going through. Her dad is dead and her mom is an alcoholic. She doesn't have any brothers or sisters. What would I be like if I were in her situation or if I'd been through all the things she's been through?

Oh, Dear Father God, Please be extra close to Alissa right now. Shine Your light into the hurt and darkness in her life and make it so that she can see You and call out to You and trust in You. Please break through the powers of darkness that have a chain around the secret place in her heart. Break through and shine Your light there. I want her to come to know You. Amen.

## December 29

DSF,

Today was one of those battles with my controlling aunt when she took me shopping and wanted me to get my hair cut again like she talked me into doing last summer. I didn't get it cut. Then my aunt and I got into an argument at the restaurant when she said she thought Alissa was so perfect and she thought I should try to be more like Alissa. I blurted out that Alissa was pregnant and asked my aunt if that's what she wanted for me, too. She got SOOOO mad! But that's another story.

What I wanted to write down were the words to this song I kept singing over and over in my head, like a prayer when we were at the hair salon. Here are the words:

Touch this heart, so full of pain,
Heal it with Your love.
Make it soft and warm again,
Melt me with your love.
I don't want to push You away,
Come back in
Come to stay.
Make me tender, just like You.
Melt me with Your love.

I wish I could be soft and tender all the time. Oh, and I should tell you what happened after we got back from shopping. Doug was here at my aunt and uncle's and he said my hair smelled like green apples. Then he leaned over in the front of my aunt and uncle's house to smell my hair, and at that exact moment, Todd went driving by in his old VW bus!!! I'm pretty sure he saw us. I wish Todd would have stopped. Then he would have seen there's nothing going on between me and Doug, really. I'm sure it didn't look that way just driving by.

If Todd stopped, then he would've heard Doug tell me he was going to take Tracy out. I was really happy about that because she likes him and if Todd finds out that Doug is going out with Tracy then he won't think I was trying to get Doug interested in me while we were ice skating.

# January 1

Happy New Year, Dear Silent Friend!!

What a New Year's Eve I had last night! Where do I begin? First, my aunt tried to surprise me and invited Todd to come to their house for a fancy New Year's Eve dinner. I didn't know he was there so when I walked downstairs and heard someone playing the mandolin in the living room, I thought my aunt had hired someone to play music while we ate. I know, that sounds crazy, but if you knew my aunt, that's exactly the kind of thing she would do.

When I saw that it was Todd I almost screamed! He told me earlier he had plans for the evening and I thought he was going out with another girl. I never guessed the plans were with me!

After the fancy dinner, we went to Heather's house for the party and on the way I told Todd about Alissa and the baby. He's sure that the baby is Shawn's, which shocked me. I hadn't tried to figure out who the father was.

Then Todd said the most amazing thing. He said that even though what Shawn and Alissa did was wrong, they created a human life and that life had something that was going to last forever—a soul. And then he said, 'Even angels can't do that.' That really stunned me when I thought about it later. I will never think of people the same way again. Every human has a soul. And every soul will last forever. Where that soul spends eternity depends on how they choose to respond to God. I'm still amazed by that thought.

But anyway, I have something else to tell you. When Todd and I left the party, we were driving back to my aunt and uncle's in Gus. (I told you about Gus, didn't I? Gus the Bus? Todd's old VW van?) We finally got to talk about 'us' and we both were saying that we wanted to be the kind of friends who were friends forever and then Todd stopped at this intersection. He pulled me out of the van and when we stood in from of the headlights, I realized it was 'our' intersection! The place where we stood last summer when he kissed me goodbye when I was leaving to go back home to Wisconsin.

I was laughing and telling him this was crazy and then he gave me this bracelet! It's so beautiful. I love it! It's a gold ID bracelet with the word 'Forever' engraved on it. That's when he told me that no matter what happened in the future, we would always be friends forever.

I'm smiling so big right now. I've never felt like this before in my whole life. And I think part of the reason is because I feel as if this bracelet represents more than just Todd and my forever friendship with him. Every time I look at this bracelet, it will remind me of the eternal part of me that's going to go on forever. My heart and soul belong to God and I am His forever!

# January 14

Dear SF,

Do you know what today is? It's Todd's birthday. I know. I didn't know it either. I can't believe I never asked him when his birthday was. I feel really bad because I didn't get him a card or anything. I found out it was his birthday because Doug called and said they were going to have a party for him over at Tracy's and he asked if I could go up to Newport Beach for the party. It's an hour and a half drive to my Aunt and Uncle's house, which is near Tracy and Doug and Todd. I was so upset because I couldn't work out any way of getting up there and my aunt and uncle are going away this weekend so I'd have to stay at Tracy's and my mom didn't think that was a good idea. So I'm not going.

My parents let me call Todd and talk to him for a long time after school today. I spent the first ten minutes apologizing. Todd, in his usual ultra-casual way kept telling me to not worry about it. I told him I hoped we could see each other again soon and he said he might be able to come down here next weekend. I sure hope it works out! If he comes, maybe I can bake a belated birthday cake for him or give him a present then. But what? Guys are so hard to buy for.

Remember when I didn't know what to get for Rick or Todd for Christmas? Well Rick has done a good job of avoiding me lately. I think he's going out with one of the cheerleaders.

*February 19*

Dear Silent Friend,

You know how some people have a bad Valentine's Day? Well, I've had a bad Valentine's week! Katie talked me into making a Valentine for Todd. Have I told you about Katie? She's my closest friend now and she's a lot of fun. She usually has great ideas. Except for this Valentine idea.

Should I tell you? Okay, but don't mock me. I've had enough humiliation for one week. I wanted to get something nice for Todd to make up for not getting him anything for his birthday. Katie convinced me to write Todd a little message from those sugar candy hearts that have the words on them. I glued candy hearts all over the top of this little box. The messages on the hearts formed a sentence. It said, 'Be True,' 'My Pal,' 'Call Me,' 'Can't Wait,' 'Your Gal.'

I know. It sounds really silly, but they don't give you a whole lot to work with on those hearts. Just a few words.

I wrapped it up in red and white heart tissue paper and put it in a box and sent it off to Todd a week before Valentine's Day.

So do you think 'My Pal' called me? No. I waited all Valentine's Day for a call. No call. I didn't expect him to send me a card. But I thought maybe he'd call. I waited five days for him to call and got more and more depressed each day.

Today I was over at Katie's and she convinced me to call him. I haven't heard from him in two weeks and with Todd, unless he calls me I have no way of knowing if he was just busy or if he was unconscious in some hospital somewhere.

So I called, and he answered on the second ring. He acted like nothing was wrong. He talked about how the waves were up for the winter swell and how he went surfing this morning. After about four minutes I finally asked if he got my Valentine's present and he said, 'Yeah, but why didn't you just put the candy hearts inside the box? I had to peel off the glue before I ate them.'

I practically screamed in the phone at him! You should have seen my face! Katie was fanning me as if she thought I was going to pass out. I must have gotten pretty red.

Can you see why I said it was a disaster of a Valentine's Day? No cards. No call. And Todd ATE my secret message!

Now Katie is telling me I need to think of a better idea for an Easter present for Todd and I'm telling her I'm not in the mood to lay any more eggs, decorated or not!

*March 28*

Don't have much time, DSF,

But wanted to write down the words to a song I heard today before I forget it. I don't remember all the words, but here's part of the song:

> You never gave up on me
> Your arms are still open
> Waiting for me
> So here I come,
> I got your invitation
> Here I come
> No more hesitation
> Here I come
> Back to your heart again.

It has a really pretty tune. It made me think of God and how He's always waiting for me with open arms. He's my Valentine every day of the year.

By the way, it's a week until Easter and I decided not to send anything to Todd. He's been calling me a little more often and I think he might come down here to Escondido to see me during Easter vacation. But it's an hour and a half drive each way. I don't know if ole Gus is able to come this far.

I've begun to realize that this really, truly is a friendship with Todd. It's not a boyfriend/girlfriend thing, even though he gave me the bracelet and kissed me and everything.

In some ways I wish he hadn't kissed me because that makes me think it's more of a boyfriend/girlfriend relationship. But his kisses, both times—when he gave me the flowers and when he gave me the bracelet—have been short and sweet and not like a mushy movie kind of grab-her-and-kiss-her-good kind of kiss. And they weren't pushy kisses like Rick's two kisses were.

I wonder what kisses mean to Todd? I think they mean something different to him than they do to Rick. Maybe I'm making more of all this than I should. Todd's and my relation-ship, or should I say friendship, is so eternally knit together and at the same time it's held really loosely. I can't figure it out.

Oh well. I've gotta' fly. My dad is taking us out to dinner for my mom's birthday and I think everyone is about ready to go.

## April 10

Dear Silent Friend,

I haven't told you yet but I'm going to try out for cheer-leading. I've been swamped with school stuff and church ac-tivities and now cheerleading practice. I talked to Todd about it and he thinks if I do this, I should do it for the Lord because if I become a cheerleader, I'll have an audience. People will be watching me and watching how I react in certain situations. Maybe I should pray more about this.

Lord, I want to do this cheerleading thing for You. I know Todd's right—that if I become a cheerleader, people will look up to me and respect me. That will give me a better chance to tell them that I'm a Christian and maybe invite them to church or something. I just want whatever is best, and I want to be a good example to others.

I talked to Rick after school today. He was so sweet. Sometimes that guy can say just the right thing. For several months I hardly ever saw him. Now he's being super friendly again. I was getting discouraged about trying out for cheerleading but he convinced me I should give it my best try. He said I have 'killer eyes' and that it's because of my innocence.

I told him he makes me feel like Play-Doh and then he hugged me right when Renee, my major rival for cheerleader walked by. At cheerleading practice Renee kept giving me the dirtiest looks. I know Renee would love it if I dropped out. But I'm not going to. Not now. I'm committed.

Katie hasn't been as supportive of all this as I thought she'd be, but then all she's talked about lately is who is going to the prom with whom and so there's not much point in talking to her about anything else. I wonder if Todd is thinking about asking me to his prom. He's a senior and all seniors go to their prom, don't they?

## April 13

My Dearest Silent Friend,

Earlier tonight I thought about writing to you about this enchanted spring evening. I really, really thought tonight was going to be a memory I'd always save in my 'Todd' scrapbook of memories. And I guess I will, but not for the reasons I thought I was going to.

When Todd came for dinner tonight, he asked if we could go for a walk. We went for ice cream and on the way he held my hand and recited some verses to me from I Corinthians 13. The verses were about love and I thought he and I were having about the most romantic evening in the whole world.

Then we got to the ice cream parlor and everything went crazy. Katie came in and told me she told Rick I was going to ask him to the prom and then Rick came in and he and Todd 'met' by bumping into each other. Rick didn't realize I was with Todd so he came over and sat by me, like he was waiting for me to start talking to him as if we already had plans to go to the prom and then Todd came back and oh, man. What a disaster!

Todd and I walked home, and we had this sort of argumentish discussion and I started crying. I apologized later and Todd said I didn't need to apologize. Then, just when I thought everything was clearing up and going back to being cozy between Todd and me again, he told me he's going to the prom with a girl from his school named Jasmine!

I'm crying again, now. Sorry if my tears are getting your pages wet.

About an hour ago everyone else went to bed. It's been painfully quiet around here. I took off my Forever bracelet and I buried it along with all my romantic feelings for Todd. I put it in with all the dead carnation petals from that first bouquet he gave me. You know how I told you I've been keeping them in an old Folgers coffee can? Well, now the brown carnations and the bracelet are both buried in the deepest corner of my closet.

If I could only bury my feelings as easily so I could get some sleep. I can't sleep at all. I can't stop crying, either. I sure don't feel like praying right now. Oh, DSF. Do you have any idea how deep this hurt is?

## May 2

I haven't paid you a visit for quite some time, have I, DSF?

I just read that part I wrote about how I wanted to become a cheerleader for God, but above all, to pursue this cheerleading dream so I could be a good example of a Christian. Well, that's sure been a lot harder than I thought it was going to be. And it seems like I ended up doing it more for me than for God.

But I won! I'm on the squad. And since I am a cheerleader, Lord, I'm going to do it for You now. I'm going to let all the girls on the squad know that I'm a Christian. I'm going to be a good example of You to them and the whole school.

## May 18

DSF,

Since that last entry so much has happened. I gave up my cheerleading spot for Teri since she's going to be a senior next year and I'm only going to be a junior. Teri deserved to be on the squad. I know she would have won instead of me if she hadn't twisted her ankle at tryouts.

Todd surprised me by coming to the assembly where they announced next year's squad and he showed me pictures from his prom. Jasmine was in a car accident awhile ago and now she's permanently in a wheel chair. What actually happened was that Todd took her to dinner with their friends, but they didn't go to the dance. Jasmine looked so happy in that photo. I was ashamed of myself for being so jealous and so mad at Todd.

I'm glad he took Jasmine. I'm glad I didn't go to the prom at my school, either. Katie went with Lance and had an okay time until she ended up coming home by herself, which was pretty low of Lance to send her off like that while he stayed.

Anyway, I think things got sort of smoothed over with Rick after the whole prom mix up. He's speaking to me, at least.

## June 6

Hello, DSF!

This Thursday is the last day of school and Katie and I are going to have a party here at my house with just the two of us to celebrate. It's been quite a year. I can't believe how fast it went. I'm more ready for summer vacation than I've ever been before in my life!

## July 5

Hello, DSF.

How are you? I'm happy. I'm having a great summer, so far. We celebrated the Fourth of July at my aunt and uncle's yesterday. Todd was there and we went for a long walk together on the beach at sunset. My brother and my mom came with us, but it was still fun and kind of romantic, even though we didn't hold hands or anything.

Todd is going to Hawai'i in three weeks with my uncle which I think is totally unfair. Oh, sure, he has to help paint Bob's two condos, but he'll still have plenty of time for fun. And three long weeks of it!

Paula, my old friend from Wisconsin, is coming to stay with me for two weeks while they're in Hawai'i so I can't exactly complain too much. I'm looking forward to seeing Paula, but I'm pretty nervous about it, too. We haven't seen each other in a year and if Paula has changed at all like I've changed in the last year, then it will probably seem like two strangers trying to start all over becoming friends. Paula will be here for my sixteenth birthday on July 27th, but Todd won't be.

Sigh.

Seems like I never can have everything the way I want it.

Oh, P.S. Katie took her driver's license test today and she missed one too many on the written part so she has to go back and take the written again tomorrow. Then she'll probably have to wait a week or so before she can take the driving part. I'm half way through driver's training summer school classes and my dad's been taking me practice driving. He makes me sooooo nervous! I'll be glad when driver's training is over but then I'll be really nervous about taking my driver's test. Especially since Katie said her brother said it was easy and then she didn't pass it.

Well, one worry at a time. And right now my next worry is getting ready to go babysit. I'm glad I keep getting asked to babysit for these three families who call me all the time, because I really need the money. But the last time I sat for this little boy he was such a brat. He wouldn't mind me at all. I hope he's better this time!

## July 27

Hold this for me, DSF,

Dear Future Husband,

I turned sixteen today, and I know it may seem weird writing this to you now, but this letter is sort of my way of making a promise to you in writing.

Maybe I already know you, or maybe we haven't met yet. Either way, I want to save myself for you. I want my whole self, my heart and body and everything, to be a present I'll give you on our wedding day.

I don't care how long it takes or how hard it gets, but I promise you I won't let anybody else "unwrap" me, so on our wedding night I'll be the kind of gift you'll be happy to receive.

I know I have a lot of years ahead of me before we get married, whoever you are. That's why I want to make this promise now, so that no matter whom I go out with, I'll always think of myself as a present I want to give to you alone one day.

I also want to start to pray for you, wherever you are, whoever you are, that God will be preparing you for me and that you'll save all of yourself for me too.

I already love you.

Your future wife, Christina Juliet Miller

## August 10

Aloha, DSF!

I wrote that letter to my future husband when we were in Hawai'i. My aunt surprised us after we picked up Paula from the airport and said we were all going to Maui to spend the week with Uncle Bob and Todd. It was a dream come true, but even before we left I found myself wishing Katie was coming with me instead of Paula because Katie and I have gotten so close this past year. Paula and I tried to pick up where we left off in our friendship but we'd both changed so much. Then when we got there, Paula seemed set on capturing all of Todd's attention, which made me furious.

On my birthday we went swimming in this cove where we could snorkel and see lots of fish. I loved it! Todd came swimming out to my raft, and we talked and it was like nothing had changed between us just because Paula was flirting with him.

That was my favorite part of my birthday because the morning was a disaster and the luau and hula show with everyone that evening wasn't exactly my idea of a good time. I mean, it was a good time, but I would have been just as happy walking barefoot along the beach holding hands with Todd. At the luau they had us go up on the stage and dance the hula and it was so embarrassing.

## August 11

Aloha, again, DSF!

I had to go to the grocery store with my mom so I had to stop writing that last entry before I told you everything about Hawai'i. It's after 11:00 p.m. now and everyone else is asleep. I like summer nights like this when it's warm and quiet. My window is open and I can hear the nocturnal critters out there making all their happy summer night sounds. There's one cricket or frog or something that keeps making this one high note over and over. Maybe it's a bird. Anyway, my window is open and I can smell the jasmine from the front of the house. It's so sweet! I'd love to stay up all night on a night like this.

Now, on to the rest of the Maui trip.

The big adventure of the week was when we went to Hana and then on to some waterfalls and pools where we went swimming. Todd jumped off this bridge—his bridge. When he was a kid he went camping with his dad in that part of Maui and his dad jumped off the bridge into the pool of water below but Todd didn't jump. He decided he wanted to jump now and he did.

Later, Todd called it "our" bridge. He gave me a poster of the bridge for my birthday because it was a place that had good memories for him. Now it has good memories for both of us. I have the poster up in my room right now. I had to drive over the bridge because Todd was stung by a bee and his foot swelled horribly. He's allergic to bee stings and he had to give himself a shot but it still took a long time for the swelling to go down, so he couldn't drive the jeep and it was starting to get dark. Paula couldn't drive because she didn't have her glasses with her and so it was up to me to drive.

And I did it. I overcame my fears of driving and it became a forever kind of moment for me and Todd. I'm sure I'll always remember that day because so much happened. But when I think about it now, what I remember most is the way Hana smelled after it rained. It was a warm, earthy, freshly-washed kind of smell. I can't explain it but I miss that smell. I miss the sound of the palm trees when the wind rushes through them. I miss the fragrance of the white plumeria flowers and the sound of the ocean taking deep, long sighs and then letting them out on the shore. I miss Maui. I want to go back.

## September 19

I have a job! What do you think of that, DSF?

My first job.

And it was such an easy interview. Can you guess where I'm working? The pet store at the mall. It was Katie's suggestion. She said that since I used to live on a farm, I should get a job with animals. The thing I didn't tell Katie, or my new boss, Jon, is that I'm not particularly crazy about animals. I mean, I like them and everything, but I never was one of those girls who had her room covered with posters of horses. And when we had pets back in Wisconsin, they were just "around." I never had one precious, favorite pet that stayed in my room or anything.

The most embarrassing part of my interview at the pet store was that my dad took me and he stayed there, acting like he was a customer or something. The only problem was he didn't act like a customer. He kept looking at me while I was filling out the papers and he walked over closer when Jon started asking me questions.

The worst part was that my dad was wearing his overalls from the dairy where he works. He looked really out of place at the mall. It was embarrassing being with him, but at the same time, I was really glad he was there. I love my dad the way he is. Truly. It's a strange thing. I feel embarrassed being with him at times, but I wouldn't want him to change a bit because he's my dad. It's the same way with my mom. I wonder if anyone else ever feels this way about their parents.

## September 20

DSF, I have a headache.

I think I got it from Rick. Is it possible to get a headache from a guy? There's so much I haven't told you about what's been happening with Rick. I guess I didn't want to write to you about him because I haven't exactly figured out what's going on and I thought if I tried to write about everything, I'd just fill pages and pages of craziness.

So instead of long ramblings, here's what I know:

1) Rick likes me. That's a nice thing. I like the fact that he likes me and he's acted like he's been interested in me for a long time.

2) I like the way Rick makes me feel. It's different than what I've felt with any other guy. I can't explain it except to say that Rick makes me feel like I want to make myself a better person for him.

3) I don't like whatever it is that's happening between me and Rick right now. I don't know what to do with all the feelings. I think the only thing to do is keep going and try to be wise.

## September 26

Did I say "wise" last time I wrote to you, DSF?

I guess I did. I think I've been wise with Rick. The thing nobody ever tells you is that "wise" might be good and right and the best way to go but it can also bring an immense amount of pain.

Rick is a thief. There. I said it. He stole my Forever bracelet that Todd gave me and he traded it at a jewelry store for a clunky silver one with his name engraved on it. When I figured that out today, and he finally admitted it, I told him I couldn't go out with him anymore. It was the hugest, most agonizing scene you could imagine. I still can't believe what happened. And it hurts so much. I would sit here and tell you all the gory details, but I'm too exhausted right now. Besides, I don't think I'll have to record this day in order to remember it the rest of my life. If anything, I wish I could erase this day.

## September 27

Dear SF,

I read a poem out loud in class today and it was as if this poet, Christina Rossetti, knew me and knew all about what had been happening in my life these past few weeks. The amazing part is that she lived over 150 years ago in London, and yet, she expressed exactly what I felt. It made me think of how it doesn't matter when or where we live, women are the same everywhere and in every generation. We all share the same kinds of hopes and dreams and fears and hurts.

It's kind of long, but it's really good. Here's Christina's poem, "Twice." (And isn't it interesting that we even share the same first name? I'm definitely going to look her up in heaven!)

> I took my heart in my hand
> (O my love, O my love),
> I said: Let me fall or stand,
> Let me live or die,
> But this once hear me speak—
> (O my love, O my love) —
> Yet a woman's words are weak;
> You should speak, not I.

You took my heart in your hand
With a friendly smile,
With a critical eye you scanned,
Then set it down,
And said: It is still unripe,
Better wait awhile:
Wait while the skylarks pipe,
Till the corn grows brown.

I have to stop and make a comment here, DSF. I didn't tell you about what happened with Todd. I only reported on the agonizing break up with Rick. But there's a whole different story about Todd. Rick took me to dinner up in Newport Beach and if you can believe it, Doug was the valet when we parked the car! Doug convinced Rick that we should stop by a party at Tracy's house and Todd was there. I'd only seen Todd twice since our big trip to Maui and he's only called a few times. I honestly thought that if Todd really cared about me, he'd say something to me at the party. But he didn't. (Todd! You drive me crazy!!!!)

I stayed at my aunt and uncle's house and the next morning I couldn't sleep so I went for a lonely walk on the beach and guess who was out on the beach too? Yes. Of course. Todd!! He came and sat by me. I pulled out all the courage I had and I told Todd how I felt about him. He said I should be free to go out with whomever I wanted and that it was selfish of him to try to hold on to me and wait for me to grow up.

It was just like this poem! I held my heart out and Todd basically said it wasn't ripe. It just about killed me. Wait, here's the rest of the poem:

> As you set it down it broke —
> Broke, but I did not wince;
> I smiled at the speech you spoke,
> At your judgment that I heard:
> But I have not often smiled
> Since then, nor questioned since,
> Nor cared for corn-flowers wild,
> Nor sung with the singing bird.
>
> I take my heart in my hand,
> O my God, O my God,
> My broken heart in my hand:
> Thou hast seen, judge Thou.
> My hope was written on sand,

(Is this my life, or what? "My hope was written on sand.")

> O my God, O my God;
> Now let Thy judgment stand—
> Yea, judge me now.
>
> This contemned of a man,
> This marred one heedless day,
> This heart take Thou to scan

Both within and without:

Refine with fire its gold,
Purge Thou its dross away—
Yea hold it in Thy hold,
Whence none can pluck it out.

I take my heart in my hand—
I shall not die, but live —
Before Thy face I stand;
I, for Thou callest such
All that I have I bring,
All that I am I give,
Smile Thou and I shall sing
But shall not question much.

Every time I read this poem I know I'll remember that morning on the beach with Todd. I didn't tell you what happened after that. Todd told me he was going to Oahu. Yes, Oahu as in Hawai'i. He left the next day and is staying with his friend Kimo. I know I thought I would never see Todd again when he moved to his mom's in Florida. Now it really seems like he's gone for good. I wish I could tell you how I feel about that, but I'm not sure. I feel like Christina said in this poem, that I'm turning over my broken heart to God and I'll wait on Him and trust Him.

*October 22*

Dearest, Kindest, Gentlest of All Silent Friends,

I think you'd like my English teacher. I really like the kinds of assignments she's been giving us. First she gave us that poetry assignment where I discovered Christina Rossetti and now we have to write about friends. Maybe I should write about you! The joys of trusting all your secrets to a Dear Silent Friend.

Here are some of the quotes from the paper she gave us with the assignment:

"Friendship? Yes, please!" Charles Dickens

"My treasures are my friends." Constantine

"Friendship is rarer than love and more enduring." Jeremy Taylor

"The language of friendship is not words, but meanings. It is an intelligence above language." Henry David Thoreau

"The only way to have a friend is to be one." Ralph Waldo Emerson

"Friendship is like a sheltering tree." Samuel Taylor Coleridge

"There is no friend like an old friend,

who has shared our morning days,
no greeting like his welcome,
no homage like his praise."
Oliver Wendell Holmes

I'd like to add my own thought about friendship:

"Friends come and go, but true, forever friends are never further away than the secret corner of your heart."

Christina Juliet Miller

## November 1

Okay, laugh now, DSF, and avoid the rush.

I agreed to join the ski club with Katie and now we're going on a trip over Thanksgiving to Lake Tahoe. I know, I know. Me on skis. This ought to be interesting.

We're trying to sell candy bars to raise money for our trip and Katie keeps eating all of hers. I took some to work and Jon was so nice! He let me put them out at the cash register and people are actually buying them! I do have the nicest boss ever. He's a unique guy, but he's been very understanding lately.

## November 9

Hello there, DSilentF!

Tonight at youth group Luke asked us to write out what we're thankful for. Here's my list:

I'm thankful for my parents, this house, my health, and all the blessings God has given us, like food and clothes. I'm thankful for my friends and... I'm thankful for Todd. And Rick. And Katie. And for my job, my church, my relationship with Jesus, and the way I can talk with Him anytime and anywhere.

That's what I wrote. I was a little surprised that both Todd and Rick made the list since both of them have vanished from my life. But then I realized that what I'm thankful for is what I've learned from both of them. Not that it was always easy or fun. I'm not thankful for the pain. But I'm thankful for the experiences I gained.

## November 28

Well, DSF. I saw Rick.

He came by with Doug on Sunday. I was asleep on the couch because I was so tired from the ski trip, which, by the way, was an entire adventure in itself. First I'll tell you about

Rick. He barely looked at me. He was getting a ride back to college with Doug and since Doug wanted to stop by my house, Rick had to come, too.

I think Rick is going to be one of those guys where it's all or nothing. Either I'm completely devoted to him or I'm on his list of people to ignore. I wish it wasn't like that. That's one of the things I like about Todd. He's the same with everybody all the time. Todd takes his friendships seriously. Although, what am I saying? Todd, the great silent one—even more silent than you right now—is still in Hawai'i. I guess. Doug didn't say anything about him, so I guess Todd is still over there surfing his little heart out. I wonder if he's thought of me at all while he's been there.

Rick noticed that I had Todd's bracelet back on my wrist. I could tell he was pretty surprised about that. I wonder if he knows that I bought it back from the jewelry store where Rick hocked it? Or at least, I paid for about half of it. I don't know who made the final payment for me. I'm still mad when I think about how Rick stole my Forever ID bracelet from me.

The only good part was that Rick is hanging out with a bunch of really strong Christians and it seems they're having a good influence on him. I'm glad for that.

The strange part was that I didn't really feel anything deep inside when I saw him. I mean, I felt a little nervous, but I didn't feel all thrilled and eager for his attention the way I used to feel whenever I was around Rick or when he'd try to melt me with one of his looks. How can feelings change like that?

One thing that didn't change this Thanksgiving vacation is my friendship with Katie. It was certainly challenged a few times on this ski trip, but we ended up coming out of the experience much closer than we've ever been. I learned a lot about trusting the right people. Katie needed me to believe her and be on her side when these other girls on the trip were trying to get me to take their side against Katie. I didn't stick up for Katie at first; at least, not the way she wanted me to side with her. I wish I had. All I can say is that I'm glad she's so forgiving and gracious as a friend.

The other big event on this ski trip was that I ran into the ski instructor. I mean I literally ran into him. I still can't believe I'm such a klutz sometimes. I think I'd like to try skiing again only I'd like to go at my own pace without a lot of other people I know watching me. It was fun. I guess.

## November 30

Guess what I have, DSF?

A coconut from Hawai'i! Todd mailed me a coconut from Hawai'i and he wrote the reference to a Bible verse on it. He wrote "Phil.1:7." The man at the post office told me I got something from "Phil" and I said I didn't know anyone named Phil. It was so funny. Katie was with me and we cracked up. Then she figured out the Phil. meant the book of Philippians in the Bible. So we rushed home and looked it up and part of that verse says, "I hold you in my heart."

Is that the most romantic thing you've ever heard? Here I thought Todd was long gone and he sends me a coconut and tells me in secret, romantic and holy language that he's thinking of me. Todd holds me in his heart. Ahhhh. I hold him in my heart, too. But then, you knew that, didn't you?

## January 16

I missed you, Dear Silent Friend!

My family went to the mountains with Uncle Bob and Aunt Marti for Christmas and I wish I would have brought you with me. I did a lot of thinking and reflecting and I wish now that I had you with me so you could have taken those thoughts and held them for me. It's been two weeks now and I'm afraid I've forgotten some of the things I was thinking about then.

I just can't believe we're already two weeks into this new year. All my teachers are giving us homework like crazy! I have a paper due for history on Friday and I haven't started it yet. I ended up working extra hours last week at the pet store and it seems that as soon as I get home, I just crash. My room is such a mess. I don't like being this behind in homework and this unorganized.

And now for the big news of why I've been so busy. Todd is back from Hawai'i! He got back on New Year's Day and showed up at our party at my aunt and uncle's house with leis and hugs for everyone. He had some pretty fantastic tales to tell of his adventures in Hawai'i.

We've seen each other three times since he got back and I think all my old feelings for him are as strong as ever. His birthday was two days ago and I made him a big batch of chocolate chip cookies and I got him a gift certificate at a sports store at the mall where they have stuff for skateboards because he said his skateboard needed new wheels. It was a good choice for a gift because he seemed to really like it.

For his birthday we went to see this art exhibit in Laguna Beach, which is not far from where he lives. They had a big display of all these old surfboards and other California beach memorabilia from the past 50 years. One of the old wooden surfboards had been made into a bench, which Todd thought was very cool. It wasn't especially comfortable, but I agreed that it did look pretty cool in the corner where they had it under a fake palm tree with a set of bongo drums.

My mom was really nice. She went with me up to Newport Beach and went to dinner with Aunt Marti while Todd and I went to the exhibit. Then we all had birthday cake at Bob and Marti's and my mom and I drove home. I would have loved to have stayed longer, but I'm happy that I got to be with Todd on his birthday. I think it was one of the funnest times Todd and I have ever had. And I wouldn't be surprised if the next time I see him he tells me that he turned his old surfboard, "Naranja" into a bench like the one we saw!

## February 1

I need a new pair of shoes, DSF.

Aren't you glad I told you? I only have one pair that I really like to wear and they're coming apart on the side. I saw a pair I like but I didn't even try them on because they were too expensive. Now I have to decide if I want to try and find another pair somewhere, or if I should keep checking on this pair and wait for them to go on sale. If they went on sale for 60% off, I could afford them. But what are the chances of them being marked down that much, especially in the next few weeks? I know. I'm dreaming. I need to face reality and go find something else.

Now, if I asked my Aunt Marti to get them for me, I know she would and the price wouldn't make her blink. But I don't feel right about that. I know Marti likes to buy clothes for me and she never acts as if it's a burden. I just don't know how that makes my mom feel since Marti can afford to buy things that my parents can't afford to buy. It's more important to me that I be a good caretaker of the things I have than to collect more stuff. My parents have taught me that. My dad fixes things when they break rather than going out and buying a new one to replace it. My mom has fewer clothes than anyone I know but she always looks nice and she never complains. I think there's a sort of dignity that comes with making do with whatever you have.

But I still definitely need a new pair of shoes. Definitely.

## April 4

Do you hear the wind, DSF?

It's been stormy for five days now. Wet and cold and gray. We used to have spring days like this in Wisconsin but I don't remember having this much rain since we moved here. It's kind of depressing.

## May 28

Hello, DSF.

My life has been full of school, church, work, friends. Sorry I haven't checked in with you more. Yesterday was Katie's birthday and we had a huge party at this pizza place called Sam's. I planned it as a surprise and invited everyone I could think of from school and church. I told Katie I wanted to take her out for her birthday and that it would be my treat but all I could afford was Sam's. I don't know if she had some suspicions or not, but she went along without any complaints. I told her I wanted to see something in the back room. She followed me in and everyone jumped up and said surprise. It was great!

We had a gummy worm fight from this bag of gummies that one of the guys brought and we threw those wiggly worms all over the place. I got one in my hair and Katie got one down her shirt. The gross ones were the ones they licked to make them stick on the wall and then picked them back up again and threw at people.

Todd and Doug came and they said they tried to talk Rick into coming but he had a date. Are we surprised? Todd and Doug and Rick are all roommates in San Diego. Yes, that one is surprising. One never knows what relationships are going to come back around again. Don't be quick to burn any bridges, right?

## June 11

Dear Friend of Silence,

Tomorrow is the last day of school. My junior year went by way too fast! I think it was my hardest year as far as the amount of homework and trying to balance school and job and friends and everything. I'm feeling real melancholy tonight. It's like something is missing because I don't have anything to particularly look forward to this summer.

Two summers ago was when I came to California to stay with Bob and Marti. Last summer Paula came and we ended up going to Maui. This summer there is absolutely nothing on the schedule. Not even a family vacation. And who knows how much I'll get to see Todd since he said he's going to be working this summer and maybe taking a summer school class.

It all feels so uneventful. Katie wants to go to summer camp with the church youth group. I think that's sounding more and more like a good idea. I'm going to talk to Luke about it and see if I can still sign up to go.

My brother is playing Little League softball and he got a two-base hit last week. I think it was the highlight of his life. David is still a pest, but as he's getting older, he's getting more tolerable. I think he might turn into a fairly nice kid by the time he gets to high school. However, by then, I'll be off to college and I won't see him much. Isn't it funny that I'm even thinking of that now? And that I'm feeling sad about not being around my brother when he's in high school? I told you I was feeling melancholy.

## July 10

DSF, will you remind me to get more details upfront from Katie next time she comes up with a great idea?

I can't believe this. Katie talked me into going to camp and now she's not going. The worst part is that I thought we were going to be the campers when she dreamed up this event. But no. She signed us up to be counselors and so yours truly is going to be a camp counselor and Katie Weldon, the big flake, is staying home.

Actually, it's not her fault. And she's not really a flake. Her parents are funny about Katie being involved in a lot of church activities. When they found out the camp was a church camp, they didn't want her to go. I admire her for honoring her parents' decision, even when it seems like an unfair and/ or pointless decision. Katie has more patience than I think I would have under the same circumstances.

The thing is, when Katie submits herself to her parents' decisions, I've seen God do His "God-things" in her life. (That's what Katie calls it when things happen that you can't explain and you look back at it and all you can say is that God did that. That's why it's a God thing.) It's like God blesses Katie in a special way for her obedience. That's why I can't be too frustrated at her for backing out of camp. It's not exactly her choice or her fault and I want to support her in her difficult decision to honor her parents, (I can't believe I'm saying this) even when it's difficult for me, too.

## July 21

Back from Camp Wildwood, DSF!

You should have been there! Actually, I'm glad I didn't take you. The girls in my cabin would have discovered you the first day there, read all my secrets on your pages and then tortured me the rest of the week.

Yes, it's good that you stayed home.

It was an interesting week. That's the only word that comes to mind when I try and describe it. I learned that I'm not exactly the camp counselor type of person, although I was much better at it by the end of the week than I was the first few days. I also learned that red ant bites are about the most torturous of all experiences. I was attacked by a whole army of red ants the last day when I hid inside a hollowed-out tree stump for the camp counselor hunt. My legs were covered with bites. And I mean covered. It was awful. I spent the last night in the infirmary.

My favorite song from camp was one Doug and Todd sang when Katie and I visited their God Lovers Bible Study in San Diego a few weeks ago. It's from a verse in the Bible:

> Eye has not seen
> Ear has not heard
> Neither has it entered the heart of man
> The things God has prepared
> For those who love Him.

## July 23

Dear SF,

Katie called while I was writing my last entry and then I had to go to work so I never finished it. I wanted to write more about camp because some good things happened there. The best of all was when Sara came to visit me in the infirmary and she said she wanted to give her heart to the Lord. Here I'd been trying to "preach" at these girls all week and thought I'd failed and then little Sara decides she wants to become a Christian and she comes to the infirmary to ask me to pray with her. It was amazing.

The other amazing thing was what I learned about myself with guys. I know. I talk about guys all the time, don't I? And I don't think of myself as being boy-crazy or anything. It's just that I'm learning. And as I go along, I want to remember what I've learned so I don't keep repeating the same mistakes. The sort of mistake I made at camp was with Jaeson. I spent way too much time focusing on him and playing out a role of being his summer camp crush. It wasn't terrible or anything. The canoe ride he took me on was very fun and memorable. What I learned is that I'm so open to whatever comes my way that some stuff comes rushing in to my life and I don't discern at the moment if it's a good thing or not. I don't decide ahead of time what I want or what's important. I mostly let things happen and then I evaluate it later. I guess that's what I'm doing now.

And my evaluation is that I should have realized at the beginning of the week that Jaeson was the kind of guy who had a different girlfriend every week at camp, so that when he started showing interest in me, it was simply because I was his choice for a girlfriend for that week. If I'd realize that, I probably would have still hung out with him and gone on the canoe ride and everything, but I wouldn't have gobbled up the attention as if it actually meant anything to him.

Does that make sense? It's like it's okay to develop short term friendships as long as I realize at the beginning that it's just a blip on the screen of my life. I don't need to make such a big deal of everything.

My mom wants me to help her fix dinner tonight so I better go. She says I don't know how to cook and it's time I learned a few things before I grow up and leave the house. She says if I had to move out now, all I'd know how to fix would be scrambled eggs and toast. I didn't tell her this, but the scrambled eggs reminded me of when I made breakfast for Todd on the beach and the sea gulls came and scarfed all the scrambled eggs. I think it's about time Todd and I tried another breakfast on the beach and this time we'll keep the birds away.

## August 12

Greetings on a very hot night, DSF!

I have a big box fan aimed at me right now but it is still so hot in my room that I don't know if I'll be able to get to sleep. It's the middle of August and the weather man said on the news tonight that we broke a record today for high temperatures. On the news they said the last time it was this hot in Escondido in August was in 1934 or something like that. My hand is sticking to the pages as I write this.

Yuck! It's too hot!

My aunt has planned an end of the summer outing. She and my uncle rented a houseboat at Lake Shasta and we're going in a week and a half. Todd is coming!!!!! So are Katie and Doug. This is going to be the best trip ever! I have to admit I do love being spoiled by my aunt. She really gets into planning my social life for me and even though it bugs me sometimes, I realize what a treat it is to be able to go fun places and do fun things like this with my friends.

Todd called last night. I was saying how the future seems like such a mystery. I'm about to begin my senior year of high school and I can't figure out how I got to this last year so fast. Todd is about to start his sophomore year of college and he needs to make some solid decisions about classes and his major. Then Todd said, "I'm glad that God has plans, even when we don't, because God is 'prior.' Wherever we're going, He's already been there."

I liked that. God is "prior." He's already been there. He has charted a path for us to follow. The dearest desire of my heart is that I stay on that path and not go off on my own trail and waste any of my life on a trail that's not God's preferred choice for me.

## September 4

I only have a minute, DSF,

But I had to tell you my wonderful news. Todd and I are officially together. We had this very romantic talk our first morning at Lake Shasta and we decided the next step for us is to be a couple and to start going together. It's been sooooo wonderful!

He's coming this weekend to take me out. I can't wait to see him. We had such a great time on the houseboat. He is so amazing. I care about him more than I can say. We've come so far; waited so long to be at this next level in our relationship. I don't think I've ever been happier. I think Todd is happy, too. I feel like our relationship gets stronger the more we each grow closer to God. Isn't that amazing?

I was trying to explain it the other day to my mom and I didn't have the right words. It's a lovely mystery.

Today is the first day of my senior year and I have to hurry. Katie and I are riding together and you know how Katie doesn't like to wait for anything.

### September 8

DSF,

I'm so worried about Katie. We met this guy from Ireland the first day of school and I think she's fallen for him in a big way.

### September 17

Katie and Michael are together now. I don't feel good about this. Todd and I met them at the movies last week and we all went together and then out for pie afterwards and I really don't think Michael is a Believer. What is Katie thinking?

### September 28

Hi there, Dear Silent Friend,

We celebrated my dad's birthday today and I got him a flashlight. I know. It sounds like a really dull present, but he liked it. Todd suggested I give my dad a really personal card and so I ended up writing out the assignment I did for English where I described my dad. He read it and got all teared up. Then my mom started to cry and I got all teary eyed, too. Todd was right. He said that dads like to hear every now and then that they're doing something right. My dad really liked it.

It made me think about my heavenly Father. I don't often tell Him how I feel about Him. I know He loves me, even though I don't think I'll ever understand how much. And I love Him, even though I don't think I'll ever be able to fully tell Him how much.

Heavenly Father,

I want to take the time now to tell you how much I love you. It's not enough to just realize that I don't tell you. I need to tell you. You are awesome, God. You created the heavens and the earth and all that is in them, and yet you care about people. You care about what happens to us and more than that, You want to have a relationship with us.

Thank you God, for seeking me out and pursing a relationship with me. I love you so much. I look back on my life and see so many times when you were at work doing your God things, even though at the time, I didn't recognize what was going on. You have done so much for me.

Thank you. I love the way you comfort me and give me your peace in rough times. You provide for all my needs and so many of my wishes; sometimes even before I wish them. It's amazing to me that you care that much about me.

Thank you so much, Lord. Thank you.

## October 4

Do you like your new shelf, DSF?

Can you still smell the fresh paint? It's supposed to be dry, but when I came in my room after the door had been closed all day, I could smell the paint. I bought your new bookshelf at a yard sale last week and Todd helped me paint it at Bob and Marti's house. It fits perfectly in the corner of my room. Every time I look at it I feel warm and content inside. Just a few minutes ago I was remembering the silly little paint brush fight we had while we were painting it. See my face? I'm smiling at the memory.

Things are so great with Todd right now. He is such an amazing guy. Sometimes I feel as if my heart it so full of appreciation and admiration for him that if I added one more pinch, my heart would burst. Sometimes I wonder if this is love. How do you know if you're really in love? How much of our feelings are we supposed to figure out and how much are we just supposed to feel?

I feel deliriously happy tonight. Happy to be alive and well. God seems so close right now. When we went on the houseboat Todd and I went out in the raft the first morning and the sky was so beautiful! Todd quoted this verse in Nahum that said, "The clouds are the dust of His feet." Now whenever I look up and see fluffy clouds, I think that God has been walking across the skies.

A few months ago there was a guest speaker at church and he taught on this one verse about how the Spirit of God roams the face of the earth looking for just one person who will be obedient and faithful to Him.

That's what I think of when I see the clouds. The Spirit of God is roaming the earth again, seeking the few who love Him above all else. I want to be one of those few obedient, faithful God Lovers. I feel as if I have so far to go and so much to learn. I want to not only read my Bible but I want to study it more. I want to go deeper in my relationship with the Lord so that when He speaks in His still, small whisper I'll hear Him.

## January 6

I'm sorry, DSF.

I have neglected you. How long has it been since I slipped between your covers? Three months? I've missed you.

It's not possible for me to catch you up on everything that's been happening, but I do want to make a few "markers" so I'll remember this season of my life.

Katie and I have gone through our biggest testing time ever. Katie has a boyfriend. Michael. And she's changed. A lot. I feel as if she and I are miles apart. I've been sooooooo busy with school and work and church and Todd and my family that I haven't put the kind of effort into keeping things close with Katie. We had such a fantastic friendship. I don't want to let it go.

The other thing I want to write down so I remember is that I've been enjoying being on the yearbook staff and taking pictures. It's a lot work and a lot of hassle and this guy, Fred, drives me crazy, but all in all, I like it.

Todd has been telling me all along to pray about Katie, and I have been, but I don't see anything changing. She and Michael keep getting closer and she and I keep moving further and further apart. It's depressing.

Todd's birthday is coming up on the 14th and I don't know what to get him. He and I have talked about what to do and nothing seems to be working out. That's depressing me, too. I don't want his birthday to slip by without us being able to do something memorable together. I don't think his birthdays were ever a big deal when he was growing up and that's just sad. We have to celebrate somehow.

# May 13

Dearest Silent Friend, I'm so glad I can talk to you.

I just spent the last hour or so reading all through this diary and I'm amazed at how much my life has changed. So much has happened. I'm glad you've been there for me for all these years. You may be silent, but when I go back and read all these secrets you've held for me, it's as if you're speaking all over again into the deep corners of my heart. I see God at work in my life.

And tonight I needed to see that. I did something today that I think I'll end up regretting, or at least second guessing for a long time.

I broke up with Todd.

I know. I can't believe I'm just sitting here telling you this and that I'm not falling apart. I feel numb.

There's a reason I let go of my end of the rope in our relationship. Todd received an invitation to finally go on an extended missions outreach with a group he'd contacted some time ago. It's what he's always wanted to do. And he wasn't going to go because we're together now and things have been so great. That's why I had to be the one to break up, to let him go, because I don't think he would have done it.

I gave him back the Forever bracelet when we were at the beach watching the sunset. He crumbled to the sand and he cried. He cried, DSF! I can't begin to tell you how I feel right now. See these tear drops? They're mine. And they're only the beginning. I can't believe all this happened tonight. I'm still numb.

We barely talked on the ride home. And then he walked me to the door and turned and left. No goodbye kiss, no wishes for our future. Just goodbye!

Oh, what have I done? What was I thinking? I felt so sure this is what God wanted me to do. But why? And if it was what God truly wanted, then would it hurt this much?

I feel exhausted. I want to tell you more of what I'm feeling, but I can't right now.

## June 24

I'm writing this with a hesitant hand, DSF.

The reason I say that is because I'm not sure I trust myself to write out my feelings at the moment. They've been so mixed up the past few weeks.

Todd left.

He never called. Never said a special goodbye. He just left. Sometimes I'm sure I did the right thing. Other times, like right now, I ache, thinking that I made the biggest mistake of my life. I've plotted a hundred ways to get him back but I haven't followed through on any of my schemes.

This whole phase of our lives feels like it's bigger than me. Bigger than both of us. It's as if this is about something else. A test maybe? Is God testing us to see if we really mean it when we tell Him we love Him more than anything or anyone else? Or is all this just a self-inflicted torture that didn't really need to happen? I mean, did I really hear God? Or in a deep, unidentified way, did I really want to let Todd go? Was I feeling panicked about getting too close or about being too absorbed with Todd when I have all these other life-changing decisions to make, like where am I going to go to college in the fall? What do I want to be when I grow up?

I don't know. I'm second guessing myself on everything. I freak out for awhile and then I get this calming peace and I know that God is still in control. Let me remind myself of that again.

## GOD IS IN CONTROL

He still has a plan He's working out. He's still prior to anything I decide or anything I do. He's God.

The most confusing element of this is Doug. He's suddenly in my life in a big way as if he can now step in and take Todd's place. I appreciate all the kind attention, but I can't figure out what exactly is going on with him.

I've got to go to work. I'll scatter all the rest of my insecurities across another one of your pages in a day or two. You can hold them for me, if you don't mind. Then maybe someday down the road I'll come back and read these crazy words and it will make sense. Or maybe it still won't all make sense. But at least I'll know that in the midst of it all I was trying to trust God. Trying to understand and do the right thing.

## June 26

Hello there, DSF!

I imagine after the last few entries you might have thought that I'd never have another happy word to write. But today I do. Katie and I went to the beach together this afternoon, just the two of us and we had the best time! She broke up with Michael a couple months ago. I never told you, did I? It was around the same time that I was breaking up with Todd and I guess that took first place over Katie's broken heart.

She and I call ourselves the "widow-women" and that allows us to treat ourselves to afternoons at the beach and movies we both like to cry at with an extra large tub of buttered popcorn between us.

Next weekend my family is flying back to Wisconsin for my grandparents' fiftieth wedding anniversary. It's the first vacation we've all been able to take together in a long time. I'm looking forward to it. The only thing I'm not looking forward to is the possibility of seeing Paula. I haven't had any communication with her for so long. It's going to be very strange seeing her again.

## July 3

Dear SF.

What is love? How does a person know if they are truly in love? What makes love last? I think it's important to think through some of these things and decide what's important to me.

Tonight my grandparents celebrated their fiftieth wedding anniversary at the church where I grew up. I asked them how they knew they were in love and how they knew who was the right person to marry. They gave me several answers. Grandma says love is a one-time decision followed by lots of everyday small choices that build on that original decision. Grandpa was kind of funny. He said it has to do with what you have in common.

Here are two words I want to think about when it comes to relationships: Commitment and Intimacy.

I think commitment needs to be the foundation for any lasting relationship, just like I didn't have a deep and growing relationship with Christ until I first made a commitment to Him. With intimacy I don't mean physically. I mean knowing the heart of the other person in a special way so that you share and treasure the same things that are important to them.

I never realized it before but I want that kind of intimacy more in my relationship with the Lord. I want to share and treasure the things He values. I want to know what's in His heart.

God wants to have that kind of intimacy with me. I know He does. He knows everything I've ever tucked away in this secret corner of my heart and He wants to share it with me.

Wow! I just had one of those moments when everything seemed clear. I realized that Almighty God has chosen to be committed and intimate with me. Love is a choice, just like Grandma said. And God chose to love me. Not only one time, but over and over again even when I do things He can't stand. Wow. God chose me and He chooses me over and over again every day, regardless of what I do or don't do right. That's amazing.

## July 6

Greetings, my Silent One.

We're back from Wisconsin already and I wanted to write about something that happened there. I didn't see Paula, but I saw Matthew Kingsley. He's a boy I grew up with and had a huge crush on all through elementary school. Matt came to see me the first day I got to my grandparents. We spent a lot of time together, and talked a lot. We both were sort of trying to figure out if we still had anything left of our childhood crushes. He knew I had a crush on him. This weekend was the first time I found out that he had a bit of a crush on me, too.

We were able to talk about our feelings and thoughts openly, which I thought was great. We decided that even though we sort of feel a little something for each other, that doesn't mean we have to act on those feelings. We were childhood friends and we can now be old friends.

Our talk was all wise and mature and nice. But now that I'm home, I'm having these funny little waves of second thoughts. I mean, what if there could have been something of a long distance romance that could have budded there if we encouraged it along?

I've been thinking about it a lot today and I guess my conclusion is that when we walk with the Lord and trust Him along the way, He makes our path clear. If something was supposed to start up between Matt and me, then I believe God would have worked it out. I didn't miss any important clue along the way.

Do you want to know something I just thought of? I think I'm stuck in a pattern of "summer love." Ever since I met Todd on the beach the summer I turned fifteen, I've subconsciously looked for a summer romance each year. The summer I turned sixteen was when we went to Maui and I was expecting much more "romance" from Todd. The next summer I was a counselor at camp and I soaked up every bit of attention I got from Jaeson as if that was supposed to be my heart fling for that summer.

This summer, I'm "single" so of course I was expecting something poetic to spring from being reunited with Matthew. This could be a dangerous pattern. The funny thing is, I have to stop writing this now because I can hear Doug at the front door talking to my dad. He and I are going to a concert at my church tonight. Here I am scanning the list of potential candidates for a summer romance when there's one really "awesome" guy waiting for me in the living room right this minute!

## July 31

Oh, my peculiar treasure, my dear Silent Friend,

I've been crying for the last hour. You can't imagine how deeply I've been hurting all day. If a heart can bleed, I know mine is bleeding right now. I turned eighteen on Tuesday and everything was wonderful.

Then today I was looking for something in my top drawer and I found a picture of me and Todd and I just started crying. Doug took the picture of us at Disneyland last summer when we were on the canoe ride. I put it in a heart frame that Todd bought for me at Disneyland because he said he wanted to buy something special for me. When we were in the gift shop, Todd said, "Do you see anything else you can't live without?" and I said, "Yes. You." Todd said, "You could live without me, Christy." And I said, "But I wouldn't want to."

That's when Todd took my face in his hands and kissed me in the middle of the gift shop! There were tears in his eyes. He held me tight and whispered, "If you only knew, Kilikina. If you only knew."

I didn't know what he was talking about but I remember feeling panicky as if something was wrong. Todd and I went on a long ride on the river paddle boat and we talked for a long time under the stars. He told me about his childhood and how I was the first person who cared so deeply and consistently for him in his whole life.

I'm crying again now as I remember his face. It was only a year ago, but it feels like a lifetime ago. I've been laying here on my bed, looking at this picture of Todd and thinking that if what he and I had was only for a season, it was worth all the ups and downs and joys and heartaches. Knowing Todd Spencer was a precious, peculiar gift from God. I guess I wanted it to last forever, just like the inscription on the bracelet he gave me.

But even that bracelet is gone now, too. Todd has it. Or maybe he's sold it or given it to someone else. I have no way of knowing. He doesn't write to any of us from the old gang.

Doug is coming over tonight and he's taking me out to dinner as a belated celebration for my birthday. Doug is such a good friend. I appreciate him. We just hang out together and talk. He doesn't mind if I talk about Todd. Sometimes I remember fun things Todd and I did and Doug jumps in and tells me stories of funny things that happened when he was hanging out with Todd, before I met either of them.

Okay, I've stopped crying now. I think I needed to have one last final goodbye cry over Todd. I need to put away all my memories of him so I can move on. The torture for me is wondering if he's thinking of me. Did he forget about me right away? Has he met someone else? Does he ever sit and look at an old picture of me and cry a little too?

I guess I'll never know.

A few days ago I was reading in II Samuel 12 about how King David was in deep mourning when his baby was sick and dying. Then when the child died, he "got up, washed his face, went out and worshipped God." Everyone asked why he went back to life as usual after being so upset.

I underlined what David said. I know it doesn't exactly apply to me and Todd, but it helped me a lot.

"Can I bring him back again?
I will go to him but he will not return to me."

I know that meant that David would one day go to heaven and be with his child because the baby couldn't come back to earth to be with him. But it helped me to think that there's nothing I can do to bring Todd back into my world. We'll be together forever in heaven! I actually find a strange peace and hope in that promise of God.

All I know is that for now, I need to get up, wash my face and go out with Doug tonight. And maybe it's time for Doug and me to talk about something other than Todd.

## August 7

You won't believe this, DSF!

Katie got a speeding ticket today! She had just dropped me off at home and was hurrying to get to her house before her latest favorite TV show started. (I don't remember the name of the show, but I should since she keeps telling me to watch it and I haven't watched it yet.) She was pulled over four blocks from her house and she told the officer she was sorry and she asked him to forgive her for breaking the law! Doesn't that sound like Katie?

She said he looked at her funny and said, "Apology accepted. I'm still writing you a ticket." Then Katie said, "By all means, write the ticket. I deserve it. And I appreciate the fact that you are making sure that Escondido is a safe place for us to live and drive."

Then you won't believe what happened. The officer ordered her out of the car and made her take a sobriety test! She passed, of course, and wisely decided to stop trying to carry on a pleasant conversation with him. She took the ticket and got home in time for the last 10 minutes of the show.

Never a dull moment with Katie! How boring my life would be without her.

## December 1

Happy Thanksgiving, DSF!

Thanksgiving was actually last weekend, but I'm about a week behind on everything lately. When it comes to checking in with you, I'm more like a few months behind. The end of the summer zoomed by and then I started classes at the community college and it's been non-stop with work and homework and Doug. Doug and I are sort of going out now. About a month ago he and I had a long talk and he said it would help him if he knew where he stood with me. I told him there weren't any other guys in my life and there hadn't been for many months. I think he was assuming that I was hanging out more with the college group from my church since so many of them go to the same community college I go to. I do hang out with them all the time at school and on weekends, but I'm not really close to any of the guys in the group.

So Doug asked if we should consider ourselves as going together. It was hard for me to answer right away because all I could think about was Todd. I know. I need to stop that. But a year ago Todd and I had the same sort of conversation when we were on the houseboat at Lake Shasta. Todd and I decided we wanted to take the next step of commitment in our relationship, which meant letting people know that we were together.

It was so different when Doug and I talked about it. There wasn't anything romantic about any of it. We were in the cab of his truck, sitting in the driveway and my feet were cold because we'd gone ice skating and my feet were still wet. The ice skating was VERY fun! Doug is a great skater and ice skating is about the only sport I can do sort of okay. We had so much fun! I think that's why Doug decided to have the "going together" conversation when we got home. Holding hands and skating together was a lot cozier than how things usually are when we get together.

I pushed the warm memories of Todd away and told Doug yes.

Life can be strange and wonderful and mysterious all at the same time, don't you think? But still, I'm wondering… do you think I did the right thing?

## December 11

Is this wacky or what, DSF?

We're going to England! Do you want to come, too? I'll bring you, I promise. Doug organized this short-term missions trip for a bunch of us and we're going in about two weeks! I have so much to do before then.

At this point it's only me and Doug and Katie and Tracy. There might be some more people from the God Lovers Bible Study who end up coming. I'm so excited! Doug said we'll be staying in an old castle in northern England for our training during the first week. That part will definitely be a dream come true for me. I've always wanted to go to Europe and I've always wanted to stay in a castle.

Doug told me about a school in Switzerland that is connected with an orphanage in Basel. I applied to go there last month but I wasn't accepted. I was pretty disappointed, but then Doug found out about this mission in England and he pulled the whole trip together.

I got one of my Christmas cards returned today. It was the card I sent to Alissa. Remember her? I sent it to her grandmother's address in Boston and it came back saying "no longer at this address." I prayed for her for a long time today. I hope everything is going well in her life. The last time I heard from her was a year ago at Christmas. I really haven't been very good about writing to her. I guess I shouldn't be so critical of Todd never writing. I sent a Christmas card to his dad's address in Newport Beach. The card didn't come back, but I have no idea if Todd ever received it.

## January 8

Buckle up, Dear Silent Friend!

The adventure begins! I'm on the plane now, between Doug and Katie, and we are actually flying to England. I still can't believe this. I feel as if everything in my life has been rushing past me these last few months, and I'm caught up in the current.

My dad was right in urging me to make some decisions about the future. I don't know if I like being grown-up. And when did that happen, anyhow? I must be grown-up if I'm on my way to England. I can't believe I'm in college. Sometimes I feel so independent, and other times I wish I could go back to the simpler days when I would spend the whole day lying on the beach, doing nothing but watch Todd surf. Oops. I did it again; I mentioned the "T" word. I wasn't going to do that anymore.

## January 11 or 12 (Not sure, exactly!)

I'm back, DSF.

I got interrupted before and I didn't want anyone "eaves dropping" on what I was telling you.

We're on a train on our way to Lancashire, which is somewhere in northwest England. Everyone is asleep but me. I love the countryside, even though it's all shrouded with a winter frost. I'm warm and cozy inside this comfortable train. If we make our connection in Manchester, we should arrive at Carnforth Hall before dinner and in time for the opening meeting of our outreach training.

How can I describe London? What a huge, ancient, modern, bustling, polite, quaint, crowded, exhausting city! Two days were not enough to make its acquaintance. We did finally see the crown jewels at the Tower of London, like Katie wanted, and it was pretty interesting. My favorite part was climbing to the top of St. Paul's Cathedral and looking down on the city. St. Paul's is such an incredible church. I've never been inside a huge church like that before, and it makes me feel full of reverence and awe.

I found these words etched on stone at a church we visited in London. I don't remember which church. I didn't write that down when I copied this: "May God grant to the living, grace; to the departed, rest; to the church and the world, peace and concord; and to us sinners, eternal life." To that, I want to say amen.

## January 13

Dear Silent Friend,

Katie has been changing before my eyes. At first she was so impetuous about everything. Is that the right word? In London she seemed loud and determined and kind of rude. But then she said she saw the way she was acting and she wanted to change. And you know what? She did. She went from being freaked out about all the cultural changes to being open and intrigued and eager to learn. I wish I could be that teachable.

There's a girl on our team named Sierra. Isn't that a pretty name? I like it. I like her, too. She's every inch an individual and free spirit. It's funny how I'm always so in awe of people who have that kind of personality. Katie and Sierra are both the kind of people who aren't afraid to show their emotions. I wish I could be more like them.

## January 14

Yes, I know what day it is, DSF.

And maybe that's why I just had to check in and tell you what I'm feeling. It's Todd's birthday and I can't even send him a card because I don't know where he is. Do you know it's been over eight months since I last saw Todd or heard anything from him? It's like he disappeared. I imagine he's in a jungle some-where on some remote island right now. I can see him sleeping in a hammock every night, shaking coconuts from the trees for his breakfast and loving every minute of it.

I miss him. But I'm happy for him that he's doing what he always wanted to do. At least I think I'm happy for him. I would also probably be mad at him for disappearing, if it weren't for the fact that my emotions are all rather occupied at the moment.

I had a long talk with Doug on this little bridge on the grounds here at Carnforth Castle and we both realized that we weren't really suppose to be "together." I don't know why it took so long for all of us to figure that out. It never was like there was anything extra special between us. Sierra even sug-gested to Tracy that she and Doug would make a great pair and Katie had to tell Sierra that Doug and I were going together! That's when I realized that if people didn't realize we were together than maybe we didn't want them to know for some reason. Maybe we were going through the motions and our hearts weren't in it. The chemistry wasn't there beyond just a close friend level.

Doug said something like I was a goal and once he got me he didn't know why it was so important to him. That wasn't what he said, but that's how I interpreted it. The thing is, Tracy has been patiently waiting for him for a very long time. They're together now and that's as it should be.

So happy birthday, Todd, wherever you are. I miss you.

## January 19

Do you feel the bumpety-bump of the train track, DSF?

We're on our way to Spain. Just you and me. Well, and Jesus, too. The mission director asked me at the last minute if I would come here and I don't know why I said yes. I was all set to go to Ireland with Katie and Doug and Tracy.

I think I know what I'd like to be when I grow up. Or should I say, what I think God would like me to be when I grow up. I'd like to be missionary. Here. In Europe. I like working with children. Surely there's some place that needs a missionary to tell the little kids about Jesus. Whatever it takes in schooling or training, I want to go after it wholeheartedly when I get home.

# January 20

I'm still here on the train, DSF.

It's been pretty scary traveling alone. I've felt God's presence closer than ever before. But I still feel a little unsure of everything. I've been looking in my Bible for a verse to call my own. That's what one of the guys on another team here told me to do. I like this one:

"...We will tell the next generation
the praiseworthy deeds of the LORD,
his power, and the wonders he has done" (Psalm 78:4).

This one is good, too:

"Teach me your way, O LORD,
and I will walk in your truth;
give me an undivided heart, that I may fear your name.
I will praise you. O Lord my God, with all my heart;
I will glorify your name forever" (Psalm 87:11-12).

I really like that one in Psalm 87 and the part about an undivided heart because even though I don't know what lies ahead, I know that I can trust God for whatever He has planned for me. And right now, that's as comforting as a thick blanket wrapped around me on this cold winter morning.

## January 22

Do you hear that, DSF?

It's a sound I'm beginning to love. It's the sound of the ocean breeze in the tall palm trees outside where I'm staying here in Castelldefels. It sounds like the trees are clapping. They've been clapping ever since I arrived at the train station. I wish you could have seen what happened. But how could You? I had you zipped up inside my bag. When we got off the train did you hear a certain deep voice call out "Kilikina!"? And did you hear me cry out with shock and joy,

"TODD!"

Yes, Todd was here in Castelldefels!!! He's been here all along. Only I never knew that. The mission organization he joined is the same one that I'm with on this short-term trip. They put Todd through leadership training and determined where he would best serve, and they decided it was here, in Spain rather than some island in a remote corner of the world. Can you believe it?!?!

Todd was late coming to meet me but he had a good excuse. He had a hard time finding the flowers he brought me. A big bouquet of white carnations—just like the ones he gave me the summer we met. I was so shocked to see him, but he wasn't shocked to see me because they told him I was coming.

He arrived with the carnations AND a certain gold Forever ID bracelet, which he put back on my wrist. I'm wearing it right now and it makes me smile just to look at it. So many memories. This is all such a huge God thing that I think I'm still in shock.

I realized when I ran my finger over the engraved word, Forever, on the bracelet, that the true forever part about this bracelet is not just Todd's promise to always be my friend. The real promise for forever is between me and God. Friends come and go. Life changes every day. But God promised He'd never leave me. He never changes. Jesus Christ is the same yesterday, today and forever. I read that somewhere in my Bible.

Anyway, Todd and I rode in his very tiny car back to the mission house and Todd introduced me to everyone. He kept saying, "This is Christy. My Christy! The one I told you about!" Inside I was screaming and laughing and crying because all this time he's been gone I thought he'd forgotten about me. Every time he's gone away I always expect the worst but Todd's never changed in his steady insistence that he is going to always be my friend no matter what.

Everything has been a wild blur since then. We only have four more days together and then I go back to Carnforth Castle in England and meet up with the rest of the teams.

## January 25

My Dear SF,

Tomorrow I return to Carnforth Castle, and I'm a mess thinking about leaving Todd again. I feel angry. Like, why did I get to see him again only for us to be torn apart once more? What are we supposed to do next?

## February 4

DSF,

Where should I jump in? How can I possibly summarize what's happened?

I'm back home in Escondido. Back from England. Back in classes at the community college. Back to my job at the pet store. Life is normal again. Only I'll never be normal again because I've been to Europe. I saw God do amazing God things. I got to be with Todd. And now I'm home, in my same room, on my same old bed with the same old bedspread and the same dusty rose bookshelf Todd helped me paint so long ago.

What's going to happen now? I don't know.

Todd and I only were able to squeeze in one sort of long, heart-to-heart talk. We decided that we're back together. We both think it was a miracle that God brought us to the same place in Spain and the whole time we were together, we were a great team. Our feelings for each other are still there and we think they're stronger since we both know what it's like to be apart from each other for so long.

That's what we decided on the train from Spain back to England, when we had some time away from the rest of the team. Todd decided to travel back up to England with us, which was really, really wonderful because you know how distraught I was over saying good-bye in Castelldefels.

I've got to run out the door, DSF. I'll finish later.

## February 11

Howdy, DSF!

A week and a half has passed since that last entry. Life is flying by at such a fast pace around here.

Let's see. Where did I leave off on the Todd saga? Oh yes. We decided we were going together again. I had the bracelet, we were happy, it all seemed great.

Then we went to the castle for the final few days of the conference. It was great fun to hear from all the other teams and to be together with Doug, Tracy, and Katie again. And do you remember Sierra? She fit into our group as if she'd been with us from the start. It was really wonderful.

Our little group returned to London for a day before we flew out and Todd came with us. I was so tired I ended up sleeping on his shoulder on the train ride all the way to London. We stayed at a boarding house near the Chelsea district. It's run by a woman who is associated with Carnforth Castle, so she was very gracious and didn't charge us anything to stay there. (But we left a good amount of money on the dresser for her.)

Anyway, when we got there, Todd and I took off from the others and walked for a long time, just holding hands, walking and not saying anything. It was cold but there were some sun breaks and it wasn't as foggy as it had been when we were touring around a few weeks earlier.

When our fingers were finally too numb, we went into a bakery and sat in the back corner in a small booth. We ordered a pot of tea and some scones. It was kind of like the tea time I'd had with Tracy a few weeks earlier only this time it was Todd sitting across from me. Never in a million years would I have pictured the two of us in London sharing tea. Our most exotic date yet!

We started talking about our future and I was the one who questioned how practical it was to say we were going together. I remembered some of the things I'd written here after my grandparent's anniversary and commitment was the issue that kept coming up in our conversation.

I asked Todd how we could possibly be truly committed to each other when he was already committed to the mission for another year and a half. Then he said his commitment was really only for another month and the mission director had announced it incorrectly at the last group meeting. That was a huge shock to me! They're restructuring things in Spain and Todd was part of the temporary team who was there for the transition period. It's too long to tell you our whole conversation, but our final decision was to settle ourselves back into our regular routines and be committed to the things we'd already made commitments to and then pick up where we left off when Todd comes home. He might be home in a month or he might be asked to stay another year.

Todd even had a verse for us to think about. (Typical, huh?) It's in Psalm 15. It's about living a blameless life and it talks about how good it is to "keep a promise, even when it hurts." It definitely hurts deep in my heart for us to be apart but I see this as a chance to honor God and keep all my other promises to school, work, etc., even though it hurts that I don't get to do what I want to do, which is, of course, to be with Todd.

At first I thought it would be impossible to go back to a normal schedule after being with him. But here I am, full speed ahead with school and work and church and my family and it actually feels okay. I don't ache over Todd the way I did before. It feels more like a long stretch between when we can be together. It's not a break up with the agony of wondering if we'll ever see each other again. It's not great, mind you. But for now, I think I can do this.

95

## March 19

Dear Silent Friend,

I've just returned from a communion service at church. I didn't want to go at first because I was tired, but I'm so glad I went. They had a dramatization of the Last Supper. I got all choked up when they showed Jesus washing the feet of the disciples. He demonstrated His love by serving. That really struck me. I can love others the way Jesus loved them by serving them. I can make myself available to do even the most basic, servant-like tasks and in that expression of serving, I will be loving.

When we came home, I did the dishes without being asked and then I took the trash out, which is usually my brother's job. I know those are minor things, but I felt so good about it because my heart was set on serving.

## April 2

Yippee, DSF!

Todd is coming home! That was fast, wasn't it? I really expected him to call and say he was staying another year. But he's coming home to finish school before make another long-term commitment to missions. He was taking a correspondence course, but time got away from him and he never finished so he didn't get any of the credit. He's planning to go back to a university near where his dad lives and try to click off some of the necessary units. He's been all over the place as a college student and is little more than halfway through what he needs to graduate. I wonder if this is a pattern in his life. Will he always take this long to finish things?

He's on the plane right now and will arrive at LAX tomorrow morning. I can't miss class to go meet him at the airport, but I hope to see him by this weekend. I can't wait!

## April 12

Happy Easter, DSF!

What a week! I went up to Newport Beach and Todd was waiting at my aunt and uncle's house. I ran to him when I saw him standing in the kitchen, and I'm not exaggerating when I say I threw my arms around him and burst into tears! I thought I was at the point in my life and in our relationship where I could control my emotions a little better, but I guess not! It was sooooooo good to see him! This is only the second time I've seen him since he got back from Spain. He is such a wonderful guy. I feel all warm and squishy inside just thinking about him now.

Unfortunately the whole week wasn't warm and squishy. Sierra and her older sister, Tawni came down, too, which was fun. But it made for a crowded, full week. I guess I'm more of an introvert than I realized. I like all my good friends and I love spending time with them but I guess I'd dreamed up a different picture of the week. A picture that had just me and Todd in it and everyone else faded into the background.

But I have to tell you, something very tragic happened. Uncle Bob tried to start up the barbecue and it literally blew up on him. Todd burned his arm badly while trying to help him and Uncle Bob ended up in the hospital and his burns were serious. It was so scary.

My mom came up to be with Marti and there were a lot of people from the God Lovers group who showed up on the beach. Todd was in pain from the burn, but he did his best to act like everything was fine. I kept reminding him to take his pain killers and he ended up getting irritated at me. It wasn't the best of times.

But I'll tell you what was the best of times. And this is a miracle. My Uncle Bob did some soul searching while he was in the hospital and he turned his life over to the Lord!!!!! I have prayed for this to happen for so long! Bob has been going to a men's Bible Study with Todd for awhile and he said the men from the group came to see him at the hospital and that's when he realized something was missing from his life.

The other big news is that Tracy and Doug got engaged! Doug asked her in such a typical creative Doug fashion. He hired an airplane to fly across the beach with a banner that read,

"Tracy, will you marry me?" Of course she said yes. I'm so happy for the two of them. They are great together.

I just reread the last few paragraphs. Does it sound like I make all this stuff up? My life is so bizarre sometimes! My uncle became a Christian. Doug and Tracy are getting married. Todd and I are on the same side of the planet. Yes, life is good. Or should I say, God is good. Very good.

## July 23

Dear Silent Friend,

Oh, oh, oh, I am so sorry! Did you think I'd forgotten all about you? I put you in the zippered side pocket of my luggage when I went to Bob and Marti's over Easter vacation and when I got home, I forgot to take you out. I thought I'd left you at their house, so I called Uncle Bob and asked him to look for you and he said you weren't there.

Then I thought I left you in Todd's VW van, Gus. Now there's a frightening thought! But when he came down a few weeks ago I cleaned that filthy van for him just in hopes of finding you, and you weren't there! I won't gross you out by telling you all the other things I found there!

I thought I'd lost you for good. I cleaned my room top to bottom twice in search of you. Please believe me when I say I was desperately sorrowful for having lost you. I felt as if a piece of my heart had been cut out and thrown away! I thought you were lost forever!

It's been months since I zipped you away in that side pouch. At least you were dry and warm there. I haven't used that bag since then. Until today. It's the middle of the summer and I'm gathering my things to go to Bob and Marti's for the wedding of the decade (Tracy and Doug's, of course). And that's how I found you. I pulled the bag from the storage area and when I did, I felt your edges through the side pocket. Were you trying to send me an S.O.S.? You poor thing. I promise to never abandon you like that again.

Of course, I can't possibly catch you up on all that's happened since Easter in one little conversation, but let me tell you the most important news. I received a letter from a school in Switzerland and I was accepted. Yes, Switzerland! I applied months and months ago when Todd was long gone and I didn't know where he was. I wasn't accepted then and so I pretty much forgot about the school. They offer work experience at an orphanage in Basel, Switzerland, so with the work experience combined with classes, it makes for quick course work.

Last semester I took 17 units and that was almost too much while working full time and helping in the nursery at church. Then Todd came home and I suddenly had a social life again and 17 units was definitely too much.

If I go to Switzerland, I'll be gone at least six months. My parents are all for it since it's apparently an honor to be accepted to this school. But I don't know if I want to go. I heard my mom talking to Marti about it and I'm sure Marti was all for it.

I'll see Marti in three days. I'll see Todd then, too. This is a decision that needs a lot of prayer. As intrigued as I am with the delightful idea of returning to Europe, I don't know if I'm ready to be away on my own for such a long time.

## July 27

DSF, Just a quick hello!

It's my birthday and I had a pretty nice time with my family. My mom made a nice dinner and we had some birthday cake and presents. It was kind of mild but there's so much else going on. Katie and I are going up to my aunt and uncle's for Doug and Tracy's wedding tomorrow. That's why I didn't have a party or anything. Todd said he'd come down for dinner but I told him I wanted to just have some time with my family. I'm hardly ever home anymore. I think my dad appreciated that it was just the four of us. He likes Todd but my dad has this funny idea that birthdays are suppose to be private and quiet instead of big celebrations. I like both at different times.

One of the reasons I told Todd he didn't have to come down was because he was here last weekend and we were at a picnic with my parents' Sunday School class. Todd came down for the day and I thought he and I were going to go to the beach. But he found out about the picnic and said he'd rather go with my parents.

So we went to the picnic and he spent the whole afternoon hanging out with all these other families that he didn't even know, playing volleyball and even horseshoes, if you can believe that. I sat at a picnic table playing Scrabble with my mom and her friend. It was as if Todd and I hadn't even come together. When we left he was so happy and thanked my parents for the fun day.

I thought about it a lot and decided that since Todd doesn't have much of a family, he probably never grew up going to family reunions or picnics or camping trips. This is all new to him, and therefore he thinks it's fun. He has spent most of his life by himself or with his peers. Being around old people and middle-aged and young people all at the same place is a treat for him. Funny, huh?

*July 29*

Dear Silent Friend,

I'm going to Switzerland. At least for a visit to the school. My ever-eager-to-run-my-life Aunt Marti made arrangements to take me there to check out the school. She assumed Todd would go with us but Todd decided to stay home because he didn't think he could get the time off work. What's up with that? Since when did my boyfriend become responsible and dependable? Those are qualities I've always wanted in him, but why now, all of a sudden, when we could have gone to Switzerland together?

Katie couldn't go with me. That's a long story.

So I invited Sierra. Remember Sierra from the missions trip last year in England? I'm glad she was able to go. This is not a journey I wanted to make with just my aunt. Sierra is a lot of fun to be with and she'll be good at helping me make the decision of going there or not.

And yes, of course, I will take you with me. And I promise to not lock you in the side pocket of my bag. That's certainly the drawback of being a dear "silent" friend. You can't call out and tell me where you are!

## *August 7*

Ciao, DSF!

I know. Ciao is Italian, and we've been in the German-speaking part of Switzerland. But it's the only foreign greeting I could think of at the moment and everyone says it over here. We're on our way home already from Switzerland. Marti and Sierra are asleep and most of the other passengers are watching the in-flight movie. I had intended to check in with you much sooner on this journey. But you know how it goes. Especially with my aunt. It was a rather stressful, non-stop few days. The bright spot was Sierra. If she hadn't been here, I don't know how crazy I might be by now.

So you want to know if you and I are going to be living in Switzerland for a while, do you? Well, the answer is, I think so. I want to pray about it some more but I've pretty much decided this would be a very good thing in my life.

It's not as if I have to prove anything or take off and leave Todd simply because he took off and left me more than once for schooling and missions work. It's that this is a rare opportunity. Sierra told me to put it in perspective, knowing that if I ended up with Todd, we'll be together the rest of our lives. But I won't be able to pick up my life and move to Switzerland just any time I want to. She said to picture myself as an old lady in a rocking chair after all my teeth have fallen out. That's when I'll be glad that when I was young and free I took advantage of this great opportunity.

So now we're flying home and I have to find a way to tell Todd. Do you think it will be hard? Or will he be his nonchalant self and say, "Whatever you want." That's pretty much how he acted when I told him about this opportunity. He said "I'll pray that you make the right decision." Well, I hope he's still praying and I hope this is really the right decision.

## August 16

Hi there, DSF!

It's all systems go for me to go to school in Switzerland. Todd said pretty much the same thing Sierra and everyone else has been saying, that opportunities like this don't come along every day and I'll be sorry if I don't take advantage of the chance to go.

I found a verse I'd underlined a long time ago in my Bible and it gave me great peace and confidence that this was the way for me to go. It's in Psalm 107:29-31.

"He stilled the storm to a whisper;
the waves of the sea were hushed.
They were glad when it grew calm,
and he guided them to their desired haven.
Let them give thanks to the Lord for his unfailing love."

I know this decision hasn't exactly been a "storm" but I have felt tossed back and forth during this past year or so as I've tried to decide about schooling and what I want to do with my life. Or should I say what God wants to do with my life. And then you throw Todd back into that "storm" after he was gone for so long and it's been pretty unsettling.

I can't exactly explain why, but this opportunity to go to school in Switzerland has turned into a calming decision. Like those verses, it's as if God has settled all my storming about with one whisper and He is guiding me to my desired haven. Not that I ever desired Switzerland, exactly. But the seas appear calm as I now sail off in that direction.

Things are peaceful with Todd. He has a few things to tend to in his life, such as school and getting some money in the bank and deciding what he wants to do after college.

I'm not worried about our relationship dissolving like I used to worry in the past. We talked about it and Todd sees this as a season of planting for both of us. It's hard work to prepare a field and get everything planted in neat rows, just right. But now is the time to do that in both of our lives and the planting can be done better if we're in separate corners of the world. A season of reaping the harvest will come later.

## August 23

Oh, brother, DSF!

Did I sound mature and spiritual in that last entry or what? I'm glad I wrote all those thoughts down and that they were so clear then, because they are definitely not clear now! I'm dying!

This is going to be hard!

In our conversations the past two days, Todd and I have both been hinting at whether or not this is the best way to go.

But neither one of us have said, "Maybe Switzerland isn't such a great idea after all." That's probably because we both know it's the right direction for me, even if we both doubt how great it's going to be for our relationship.

Katie is the one who took it the hardest. She and I have been best friends almost as long as Todd and I have, which is what? Five years now? Unbelievable. Of course, Katie and I have had our ups and downs, too. But for the most part whenever we've been able to do something together, we do it together. She wants to go to Rancho Corona, a private Christian college about an hour from here. I think it sounds like a great school and I think she should go. She's not sure she wants to go until our Junior year so that I can go with her.

We got in this huge discussion about Katie taking the initiative to go to Rancho Corona by herself and she blurted out that she was mad that I hadn't talked through the Switzerland opportunity with her more thoroughly or sought her opinion about it. I didn't because everything happened pretty fast. So I told her I was sorry and I asked for her opinion. She said, "I think you should go."

I said, "What was that all about?" And she said, "I just wanted you to ask my opinion, as if it mattered to you. That's all."

So now I may be headed for my "desired haven" like those verses said, but believe me! The waters have not been all calm and hushed lately.

*August 29*

Oh, Dear Silent Friend,

It's been another night of good-byes. I'm at Bob and Marti's and tomorrow Uncle Bob will drive me to LAX and I'll get on a plane all by myself and wing my way to Switzerland. I still can't believe it's happening. Katie and Todd organized a going away party tonight. Of course it was here, at Newport Beach, and of course we all gathered around the fire pit and sang for hours. It was so wonderful! I can't begin to describe the torturous emotions I felt all night.

Doug and Tracy came. It was the first time I'd seen them since they got married and they both had these happy smiles on their faces the whole time. They were adorable.

Katie cried off and on all night and told me it was as hard on her as it had probably been for me when Todd left. I don't feel the same intense sadness about leaving Katie. I actually thought tonight that this might be good for her, to have me gone for so long. She's such a people person. She needs to meet new people and get involved in new groups. She wouldn't do that if I was still around.

Todd cried a little, too, when we were saying good-bye out on the patio. Everyone else had gone. Todd and I sat close on the low cement brick wall that faces the beach. For a while we just held each other and cried. We kissed three times; one for the past, he said. Then one for the present. Then a long, tender kiss for the future.

I'm crying again. I'll talk to you later, DSF. I can't write about this right now.

## September 25

Hello from Switzerland, DSF!

I've been here three weeks and I have to admit that every time I thought of writing about my experiences and feelings here on your pages, I ended up writing emails to everyone at home.

Uncle Bob was going to give me his old laptop before I came on this trip and I told him I didn't need it. Boy was I wrong! I may ask him to send it to me after all because it would sure help to not have to go to the library every time I want to work on homework or check my email.

I've written so many details to everyone else about the school and I know I'll never forget this season of my life, so I don't know exactly what to tell you.

I like it here. The program is intense. The classes are good. Every time I go to the orphanage, it rips my heart out. So many children. So much pain. You can read the suffering in their little faces. You would think in a modern world, there wouldn't be so many abandoned children. It's much harder to be around these children than I thought it would be. I'm learning a lot about myself and my ability to be compassionate.

## October 18

It's Autumn, DSF,

And it's a beautiful autumn here! I have two friends that I hang out with here at school and they also happen to be my two roommates; Amelia and Sandra. They're both from Germany but their English is perfect. They were friends before they came here so they're actually being kind to let me join in with them.

Most of the students go to the bars on weekends. Amelia, Sandra, and I usually go for coffee or sometimes to the theater. The movies are in English and you pay a different price depending on where you sit in the theater. They always sell out on Friday and Saturday so you have to go buy your ticket early.

I'm beginning to feel settled in, pretty much.

Todd has been emailing me a lot. It's really nice because he's never written to me before. Except for that coconut from Hawai'i. But in his emails now he's really opened up a couple of times about what has been happening and what he's feeling and thinking. I love having this new way of getting to know him. But I miss him so much. SO much. I should be happy, shouldn't I? Okay. I'll be happy and content with what I have, which is a lot.

## November 4

Happy "Langsam Samstag," DSF!

That means "Long Saturday." In Basel, once a month, they have langsam Samstag and all the stores are open longer so everyone goes shopping. It's kind of fun. Amelia and I went shopping for little necessities today. I stopped by a bakery that my aunt and Sierra and I had gone to last summer. I was told that every season the Swiss make different kinds of breads and cookies. I bought a fall wreath bread, and I just may eat the whole thing myself! It's so good!

Amelia talked me into getting some hot "Moroni" from the street vendors. "Moroni" are nuts. Chestnuts, I think. They roast them in a circular, metal pan that looks like a big wok. You can smell them from a block away and they smell so inviting! The vendors scoop the chestnuts into a cone shaped bag and you're supposed to walk and eat them while they're still warm.

Well, I don't know if I ever told you, but I hate nuts. I've always hated nuts. That doesn't mean I haven't tried nuts of all kinds on different occasions. I tried Macadamia nuts in Maui on my frozen yogurt. They were pretty good.

So I tried the moroni and I didn't like them. I gave them an honest try, but I could only swallow one of them. I don't know why but I just don't like nuts. Amelia ate all hers and the rest of mine.

*November 11*

Dear Silent Friend,

Can you keep a secret? Although, I guess it's not really that big of a secret. Sandra has a boyfriend. They're actually pretty serious about each other already. Amelia is sad, of course, because there isn't any special guy in her life. Amelia and I have been doing nearly everything together.

It hasn't been that great for me. Amelia and I have different interests. I'm just as content staying in my room and reading on weekends. Or going to the library and spending several hours getting caught up with my friends back home online or on video chat.

Amelia likes to go and do and see. She loves to shop. I'm certain she and I have been in every store within a 40 kilometer radius of our school. I have bought, wrapped, and mailed all my Christmas presents for home and I don't have any desire to shop again for several weeks. But Amelia is already making plans for our next shopping excursion and I'm trying to decide how to tell her I don't want to go.

# November 19

Dearest Most Silent Friend,

Do you ever get tired of holding all these thoughts for me? I'm feeling very lonely today. I told Amelia I didn't want to go shopping with her last week and she went with Jillian, a girl from Norway. Now Amelia and Jillian are inseparable and I'm alone. I thought that's what I wanted. But it can be awfully depressing when the rest of the girls in the dorm are gone and I'm the only one left.

I'm still in my sweats. It's cold today and I'm content to stay right here in my warm bed and visit with you. Although once I convince myself to get out of bed, I'm going to bundle up, go to my favorite bakery, buy something yummy and go to the library to check my emails and see if there are any from Todd.

He doesn't write as often as he used to when I first got here, but then I don't either. He's got 15 units this semester and is working 20 hours a week at a hardware store in Newport Beach. In his last email he said they'd had a big winter storm that kicked the waves up so he was planning to go surfing early in the morning like he used to do in high school. It made me homesick. I wanted to go be with him and make some scrambled eggs. Sigh.

## November 28

Gobble, gobble, DSF!

This afternoon the fourteen Americans who are at school here all got together and had a "mock" Thanksgiving dinner. I think we were all homesick and not as good of company for each other as we should have been! We had deli-sliced turkey, rolls, applesauce and green beans. It was kind of interesting to see some of the other students stop by our corner of the lounge and try to figure out what we were doing. We tried to explain Thanksgiving.

All I could think of were Thanksgivings in the past. When I was six I got sick on the candied yams and went to bed in my grandparents' puffy bed. When I was ten we had so much snow that instead of driving the eight miles to my grandparents' house, we stayed home and had clam chowder with cheese and crackers. The electricity went out at my grandparents so they couldn't cook the turkey until the next day. We ate it on Sunday after church, but it was pretty dried out.

I told one of my friends about the Thanksgiving weekend when Katie talked me into going skiing. Remember that adventure?

I wonder where I'll be next year at Thanksgiving? One thing I've learned is that God's ways aren't our ways and His thoughts aren't our thoughts. I could guess now where I'll be, but the future is really all a mystery. A faith walk. And in my opinion, an adventure worth taking.

## December 7

Oh, man is it cold here, Dear S Friend!

The snow is beautiful! But it's cold! I forgot what a winter with snow can be like. I had to buy some more socks yesterday and they're a good pair. At least my feet were warm today.

The orphanage is warm enough, which is a good thing for all those children. The lecture hall at the school here is very drafty and some students even bring blankets to put around them while they listen and take notes! I haven't robbed my bed yet but I've considered it! Amelia thinks I have "thin blood." She says it in German with dramatic emphasis and it sounds really funny.

Sandra and her boyfriend are still together. I can't pronounce his name correctly and I'm certain I couldn't guess how to spell it. Amelia and Sandra have been good roomies. They are hardly ever here, which is okay with me because I've enjoyed having the room to myself and being able to study here in quiet. It's a small room with one set of bunk beds and one bed against the opposite wall. I got the top bunk which has been good because the heat rises!

The work study at the orphanage has been a great experience. It takes a lot out of me, but it's been good. There was one little boy, Tejas, who was so shy when I first came. He's been slowly opening up and now he smiles when I come into their play area. I know that's a little thing, but it seems he's come so far. I understand now why the school asked for a minimum of a six months commitment. It would be too hard on the kids at the orphanage to have the workers change every few months. I'm pretty sure I'm going to stay through next summer. Although tonight, in this dark, chilly, quiet room, when I'm feeling so alone, next summer seems like a painfully-long time off.

## December 12

MERRY CHRISTMAS, DSF!

Christmas is actually two weeks away still, but I wanted to check in with you before all the craziness begins. My aunt sent me an early Christmas present. She sent me a ticket to fly home for two weeks during Christmas vacation. I wasn't expecting it at all. I'm excited to go home and at the same time, it feels like too much of a luxury.

You see, most of my friends here are going home but they're just taking the train for a few hours and it's not such an expense. I was invited to go to Holland with Julia, one of the girls in another dorm who I met a few weeks ago when she started helping out at the orphanage. I was looking forward to going home with Julia and experiencing Christmas in another culture. But now I feel obligated to go home.

Don't get me wrong. I want to go home. I want to see everyone. It's just that I made all my huge good-byes last September because I thought I wouldn't see any of them for a year and now I'm going to show up after only three-and-a-half months, stay two weeks and then fly back here. It's going to be strange.

But I'll see Todd. And I'm sure that will be wonderful. I've missed him in a deeper way than ever before. I think it's because we've stayed well connected, whereas when we were apart from each other in the past, I had only silence. Well, silence and one coconut.

## December 28

I'm home, DSF.

Do you recognize the familiar surroundings of this bedroom? Yes, it's ours. Isn't it strange being here? Katie has been over every day, Todd has been here five of the last seven days and my mom keeps following me around, telling me all these little details of life that I've missed out on for the past few months.

I keep thinking of the kids back at the orphanage. Julia and I bought "sweets" for each of them as a Christmas gift. One little piece of candy per child is certainly not much. Especially when I sit here with this mound of new gifts, including a brand new laptop from my uncle. I told him I was interested in borrowing his old one and instead he bought me a new one. Too much. I don't need so much.

I don't really want to say this, but it's been soooo stressful with Todd. I didn't think it would be like this. He's being more quiet than usual. Or maybe I've forgotten how quiet he can be. I tell stories about school and the orphanage and he just sits there and listens without making any comments. It makes it feel as if Switzerland is completely my experience and he's unattached to it in anyway.

Katie has been the opposite. She's like my mom in that she thinks she has to talk non-stop to bring me up to speed on every single thing that has happened since I left. And some of it doesn't interest me at all. Is it rude to say that? Katie's most exciting news is that she applied to Rancho Corona College and she's going to start in January. I'm really happy for her. I think it will be a wonderful opportunity for her.

Todd and I have plans to go to the mountains tomorrow. My brother wants to come, of course, and Katie heard us talking about it and volunteered to get a group together. Todd told both of them, "This is a day for just me and Christy."

David and Katie were both upset, but I'm eager to spend some time alone with Todd since we've been with people the whole time… but I don't like people being mad at me.

## December 29

Our snow day was a disaster, DSF!

Todd and I tried to get away this morning to go up to the mountains and dear old Gus broke down about forty miles from my house. We spent the day waiting for a tow truck, then sitting in an automotive repair shop for almost five hours while they replaced the generator. Or was it the starter? I don't know. But Gus is back on the road now and Todd and I made new plans. We were going to go to the movies but we ended up sitting in Gus in the parking lot talking and missed the start time.

We told each other how we felt and how difficult it was to be so far apart. I told Todd I thought this trip home was a mistake. It's too hard to adjust to the way things are here and know that I'm going back to Switzerland in a few days. He said he'd been trying to figure out how he could come to Switzerland so we could be closer to each other. Nothing was working out so he decided he needed to let it go and not try to force something. Then he said all we could do was let this season be what it is and enjoy it.

I agreed. Although I can't exactly say I'm enjoying this time with him the way I thought I would. When he kissed me tonight it almost felt like he was just kissing me as part of our routine and not because it was deeply heartfelt. I think he's try-ing really hard to guard all his emotions. I still think this trip home was a mistake. I don't belong here. Not now. My heart is so torn.

## January 28

It's cold, DSF.

The heater in our dorm room has been going on and off all week. We have three inches of snow on the ground outside, which makes this part of the Black Forest look especially en-chanting. I have on several layers of clothes and am under my covers and my nose is still cold!

You know, I've done so much writing on my laptop, that writing on your pages with a pen is sort of refreshing. It's a little slower and more calming.

## February 2

Not much to report, DSF,

I spend a lot of time doing emails and spend the rest of my time writing papers. Life has become a pleasant routine again here at school. After all the time I spent with Todd at Christmas the guarded feeling between us didn't go away. I still feel it now in our letters and calls. I had a much better feeling in the fall about our relationship going into a season of "planting." At Christmas it felt as if I'd turned over dry earth to check on all the seedlings I'd planted and they all looked lifeless.

## April 4

Hello, my DSF,

I've been thinking about that analogy about the seeds that I wrote in my last entry. It's been a little over two months since I wrote that. The pace around here has left little time for reflecting. We have a little break today and I went for a hike up in the hills where Sierra and I went with Alex when I was visiting the school last summer.

I went with five other students from school. We've all become good buddies. We're sort of the group of leftovers after so many others paired up with boyfriends and girlfriends during the first half of the year. Julia, my friend from the Netherlands was in our group, but about four weeks ago she and a Canadian guy from our group decided they were more than just friends and they started doing things as a couple. So the unattached ones are dwindling in number. I'm glad I haven't been interested in any guys here. It makes for such an intense relationship knowing that school is about to end and then what will happen?

Anyway, on our walk today the countryside was breathtaking. The snow is all gone. They say it all melted early this year. And now the wildflowers are sprouting everywhere.

It's so beautiful!

I picked a bunch of little yellow flowers and lacy white ones and a few blue ones. I wish I knew their names. Tatiana teased me and said, "You don't know their names? I do. That's Marie and this one is Peter." She's so funny. She reminds me of Katie—only with a South African accent. She's one of the few Christians here and we've been going to church together since last November. It's a very small church in the Black Forest about ten minutes' walk from the dorm. The service is in English at 8:30 a.m., which is why Tatiana and I go there. The congregation is a unique mix of English-speaking people of varied ages. The minister is from Wales and I love his accent.

Back to my story about the seedlings and feeling like I'd dug them up when I saw Todd at Christmas. I realized that if I'd taken this walk into the hills last December and if I'd turned up the earth, I would not have found these delicate blue, yellow, and white wildflowers hiding there. I would have found seeds. Tiny seeds, I'm sure. And they would have looked lifeless. It takes time and the miracle of God's resurrection power to bring anything back to life; including seeds and including my deep feelings for Todd.

It's not exactly like my deep feelings for him are all dead. It's more like they're buried for a season. That helps me understand why things didn't feel all bright and colorful and lively between us at Christmas. What we seemed to both be feeling was accurate for that season of our lives.

I feel so much better putting our relationship in that perspective. And glad I wrote it out so I can come back here and look at this when I feel confused again, which I'm sure I will.

## April 5

This is so cool, DSF!

You know how yesterday I wrote all that stuff about understanding that seeds look lifeless when they're in the dormant season and how that's what it felt like with Todd at Christmas? Well, you'll never guess what the message was at church this morning? It was from John 12:23-28. The pastor was speaking about how, during holy week, between Palm Sunday and Easter, Christ tried to prepare the disciples for his death. (Palm Sunday is next week.) Jesus told them, "I tell you the truth, unless a kernel of wheat falls to the ground and dies, it remains only a single seed. But if it dies, it produces many seeds."

I never noticed those verses before! It was so clear that this is God's design in many areas. Seeds have to die before they sprout and produce a bountiful harvest. Christ had to die before God could raise Him from the dead and multiply that resurrection power in the lives of Believers over and over for thousands of years.

At the risk of overly spiritualizing my relationship with Todd, (which, by the way, is something he has done since the day I met him so maybe it's okay if I do it every so often), in some ways our relationship had to die in order for God to demonstrate His resurrection power and bring new life. What I now understand is that when God brings new life, it's supposed to bring an abundant harvest. The one seed is designed to multiply its life, after it dies to itself and is resurrected.

I'm not explaining this very well, but I understand it. Deep in the sacred caverns of my heart, I understand this. My life is not to be lived just to benefit myself or even to please one other person. When I die to myself and all that I consider precious or essential to my happiness, then God brings new life and when He does, it's multiplied in order to reach many.

I wish I could explain this better. I finally understand what it is that I'm supposed to do with my life. My heart's desire is to die to myself and live to serve Christ so that He can multiply the results. It's like the last part of verse 26—"My Father will honor the one who serves me."

## April 29

My DSF,

I've been doing some more thinking about Todd. (Nothing new there, right?) Well, the thing I realized about how I've changed since I've been here is that this is the first time that Todd and I have been apart and I haven't even been interested in spending time with any of the guys here. Does that mean I'm more secure or stable or something? Could it mean what I feel deep down for Todd is really lasting and true?

He said something at Christmas that I didn't understand at the time but now I think I do. He asked if I had made any close friends here like Doug or Matt or even like Rick. I said no, I hadn't and he looked at me as if he was trying to decide if he should believe me.

I can see now why he asked that. Every time he left I ended up turning to another guy. This time I'm the one who left and I think he assumed I'd be looking for some attention from a guy during this stretch of time since he wasn't around. The thing is, I'm learning how to be content and let this season be what it is.

## May 6

Hello, Dear SF,

These past two weeks at the orphanage have been very difficult. About a fourth of the children were transferred to another center in Austria. They transferred the healthy ones who stand a good chance of being adopted. The others stayed. More than fifty new children are expected to arrive next week from Romania. This is so painful to watch. All these young hearts so eager and willing to love and be loved.

They put all the children who were leaving into one of the play rooms. I was assigned to watch over them while the orphanage staff made the final arrangements and gathered their belongings.

You know what I did? I blessed each child. I went to each one, placed my hand on their forehead and gave them the blessing Todd gave me years ago. I looked up this blessing in my Bible once. It's in Numbers 6:24. It's different there than the way Todd said it to me. I seem to remember Todd's version so this is what I said,

"May the Lord bless you and keep you.
The Lord make His face to shine upon you
and give you his peace.
And may you always love Jesus first,
above all else."

Very few of them speak English. They had no idea what I was doing. But do you know that after I blessed the first two children and kissed them on the cheek, the others silently lined up, waiting for a blessing and a kiss.

All I could think of was when the disciples tried to send the children away and Jesus stopped them and said, "Let the little children come unto me… for the kingdom of God belongs to such as these."

Oh, wow! I just looked up the reference for that verse. It's in Mark 10:14. And do you want to know what verse 16 says? I couldn't believe it. It says, "And he took the children in his arms, put his hands on them and blessed them." Jesus blessed them! He hugged them! That's what I did today, too. It felt like such a tiny gift to give them as they left, but it's what I had in my heart to give. I did the same thing for those orphans today that Jesus did for the children who were being sent away from him 2000 years ago. Amazing!

## May 14

Have you noticed, DSF?

I have only three more weeks of classes and then there's a break for almost a month before the summer session begins. I've decided to stay through the summer session because I can gain more transferable credits than I could if I went home and went to summer school there.

I've applied to Rancho Corona for the fall. Katie is already there this semester, and she's loving it. She said Sierra and some of her friends came to Rancho with Sierra's brother in order to visit the campus and decide if they want to go there in the fall, too. It's possible that Katie and Todd and Sierra and I will all be at the same school at the same time! Isn't that wild? I never would have imagined that.

I don't know what I'm going to do for my term break before summer session. I'd like to travel around, but I haven't yet made plans with any of the other students here. I guess I could travel by myself and just go visit a dozen of my friends from school since they live all over Europe. But I don't like traveling by myself very much. I did it that one time from England to Spain and that wasn't my favorite experience. It was good, but it was pretty faith stretching, too. The best part was the end of the journey when I saw Todd.

## May 18

DSF,

I'm so bummed out. I got a "D" on one of my papers for my Critical Analysis class. It's been my least favorite class here and I don't even think they have the same kind of class in the U.S. I didn't work very hard on it. It was only two pages, but it's the first "D" I've gotten here. I could write it over and the professor said he'd average the new grade with the "D" but I don't have time to work on it because all my other papers and projects for all my other classes are due in the next three weeks. Then we have a week of finals and then I'm done until the summer session.

## May 19

Guess what, Dear Silent One?!

You'll never guess. I'm going to travel around Europe for three weeks during my break. And guess who I'm going with? No, not anyone from here. Give up? Katie and Todd!

Can you believe it?! My aunt once again is delighting in playing the role of the wealthy fairy godmother. She emailed me about my plans for my break and I said I hadn't worked on making any arrangements yet because I've been so overwhelmed with all my final projects, plus we have more children at the orphanage than we've had the whole time I've been here.

So, dear Aunt Marti emails me back and says, "Don't make any plans. All has been arranged." I thought she was going to buy me a ticket to fly home for a month the way she did at Christmas and I was going to tell her no thanks. It was hard at Christmas to step in and out of my life here into my old life. I certainly didn't think I wanted to do it again when I only had the summer session and then I'd be home for good.

Then I got this screaming email from Katie. And I do mean screaming! She wrote the whole email in capital letters so it "sounded" as if she was shouting at me the whole time! Her email let me know that Marti's surprise wasn't a ticket for me to come home, but rather two tickets to Switzerland— one for Katie and one for Todd. Of course when I emailed Marti to thank her, she was so upset that Katie spoiled all the fun of her surprise.

I called my parents and talked it through with them and they're fine with the arrangements as long as the three of us are traveling together the whole time. They don't want Todd and me to go off by ourselves for any reason, but they said they trust him and they trust me. My mom got kind of choked up when she said that I was old enough to make my own important decisions and travel around and she was proud of all that I'd accomplished this year.

Todd called yesterday and he sounded really excited about the trip. Of course, he'd like to go back to Spain. Katie wants to go to Norway and I decided that more than anything, I'd like to see all that I can see of Italy. It's been a cold winter and spring and I like the thought of being in sunny Italy.

Who knows if we'll come up with a compatible plan before they both arrive here on the 6th of June. I checked out some maps and travel books from the library this afternoon. It's going to be very difficult to concentrate on my studies while those travel books are sitting in the corner calling to me.

## June 5

Our last page, Dear Silent Friend,

I'm so sad that we're on the last page. You have been my Dear Silent Friend for almost five years now. Todd and Katie arrive tomorrow. I had planned to go into Basel and buy a "sister" diary to take along on our travels, but I didn't get to it. You won't be too jealous, will you, if I share my jumbled thoughts with another diary? If I could add pages to you, I would. For all these years you have faithfully held my words, and you've invited me to come back anytime to read them. You'll never know how much you've helped me to become who I am today. You're a mirror. A treasure chest. A gentle reminder of good and bad times. And just as my Uncle Bob said when he gave you to me so many years ago, you became a real friend to me.

## June 10

Hello!

DSF, meet your new companion, your Silent Sister. Silent Sister, meet my Dear Silent Friend. I hope the two of you don't mind being joined together this way with a couple of rubber bands. It's just that I don't want to lose either of you, and I figured if you stuck together like this it would be easier to find both of you in my luggage. Sorry about the messy quarters there in the crammed bag. I didn't know that Todd and Katie would decide we should go camping with Antonio and then hit the trains to Italy.

Since I bought you in Rome, SS, does that mean you speak Italian? I guess I won't know because I'm pretty sure you'll be as quiet as DSF has been all these years.

The first thing I want to say is embarrassing, but I don't know how else to get this out. I've been acting like a brat, and I can't stop it! Everything irritates me. I keep thinking if I just get a little more sleep, or if Katie and I would stop irritating each other, or if Todd would open up more, then I'd snap out of this. But I can't seem to get back in sync with both of them. When I found out they were coming and we were going to travel around together in Europe, I dreamed about how wonderful everything was going to be. Why is it that I always over-dream?

Sorry to start off with such a downer as my first entry, but I need to figure out why I can't move beyond this bad mood. I mean, I'm traveling around Europe with my two best friends! Why do all these old insecurities have to come along? I thought I'd grown past a lot of this stuff during my time in Switzerland.

Go ahead. Say it. Tell me to breathe, to relax, to take a chill pill, as Katie would say. Tell me to stop being so overly sensitive. Tell me it's okay not to always feel like I'm in control of my life and every circumstance. Tell me I can trust God and trust my friends more than I have been. Tell me to enjoy this once-in-a- lifetime experience while I can.

Okay. You can stop there. That's enough to work on at the moment. We're going to the island of Capri, and that's stirred up all my memories of Rick because, when he was on this island on my 16th birthday, he called me. So what, right? It would only be a coincidence—if my emotions weren't so out of whack. I'm going to stop now. Maybe Todd will talk with me about some of this stuff. Something has to change. That something is probably me.

# June 14

Good morning, SS!

I have the best friends in the world. I really do. I've discovered that it takes me awhile to adjust to change. No big surprise, right?

We're on the train right now leaving Austria and on our way to Germany. I think my internal emotion-o-meter is finally reset back to someplace more in the middle. Finally! I loved our time in Salzburg. We had such a great day.

The charm of that happy city will never leave me. When we walked past Mozart's birthplace this morning, I thought of how his music still resonates here in a timeless, majestic way. The tour book said that people lived in Salzburg five hundred years before Christ was born because of the salt deposits found here. That astounds me. All Katie seemed to be impressed with was the number of fountains we found as we walked around yesterday evening. At every fountain that had a horse statue in it, she made us stop and listen to her sing, "Doe, a deer, a female deer, ray..." etc. Poor Katie tried so hard to get Todd and me to stand on the edge of the fountains and sing with her, but we let her do a solo every time.

I think all three of us finally have found a way to let each of us be our unique self and not stress over it. We have a lot of travel time left. I hope the harmony keeps up. And I don't mean Katie's singing harmony.

June 19
(I think. I'm not sure
exactly what day it is)

Hello SS,

We have been on so many trains and walked so many cobblestone streets it's all starting to mix together in my memories. I really thought I'd check in with you more often during this trip, dearest Silent Sis, but everything has sort of rolled into one long day and even longer night without much brain space left to write about it.

We're in Oslo, Norway tonight. Todd is at the ends of the earth. Really, he is. He left this morning and took a train to a Norwegian town above the Arctic Circle. Crazy? No. That's Todd. Right before he boarded the train he grabbed me and kissed me good. Katie called him "Captain Passion." She and I started talking about kisses and how Todd and I have been so sparing with our kisses over the years. I thought about it the rest of the day while Katie and I took a boat tour of the fjords.

I have so much saved up inside my soul that I'm sure it will take me a lifetime to fully express physically my love to my husband. I want to save all of that until we enter into "holy matrimony." I think that's part of what makes it holy. I think God honors virginity in a special way. When He chose to send His Son to earth, He did it through the body of a virgin. I want my marriage to be holy before God. For the first time I've begun to think that maybe I need a plan instead of just assuming that's how everything will go.

At this point in my life, I assume I'll marry Todd. But I don't know that for sure. It's as if I need to save myself from him to save myself for him.

I mean, it's not that he's coming on too strong and I have to fend him off. But I have a feeling his eagerness to do more than just light kissing when we're together is growing stronger. Well, of course it is. He's a guy, right? I feel that way, and I've always been the more reserved one.

I'm sure you're thinking that the reason I'm saying I need a plan is because I like to have things figured out so I can sort of be in control. Well, in this situation I think it's a good thing for me to plan to be in control of how I maintain my purity for my future husband, whether it ends up being Todd or not.

So here's my plan. I'm going to save my really big kisses (and everything else) and tuck them away, safe and warm in the secret place in my heart. When Todd and I are together and I feel like kissing him really good, I'll just tell myself to save that kiss. It will be like saving pennies in a piggy bank. One day I'll give that piggy bank to my future husband, whoever he is. And when he breaks it open, look out! That bank will be loaded!

## June 21

My SS,

I hereby title this entry, "In Search of the Lille Havfrue"

What is a Lille Havfrue, you ask? Why, that's the Little Mermaid, of course. As in, the so-called famous statue that my tour book said could be found in the harbor here in Copenhagen.

Yes, well, Katie and I got lost and spent way too much time trying to find the tiny statue, and when we finally located her, as Katie said, she wouldn't even turn around and look at us.

I hope I never forget the lessons I learned today. Some of the things I set out to find in life aren't as grand as I thought they would be. When those discoveries turn out to disappoint, may I always be blessed with what I had today: (1) a peculiar treasure of a friend to laugh wholeheartedly with me over the disillusionment and (2) enough money for bus fare to take me on to the next episode of the adventure.

## June 25

Oh, Dearest Silent Friend and Sweetest Silent Sister,

I have something to tell both of you. Something I have longed to write on your pages for a long, long time.

Today Todd told me for the first time that he loves me.

He loves me.

I know I don't have to record the details here because I'm sure I'll never forget the way he came to the bakery in Basel and surprised me when I thought he was on his way to the airport with Katie to go home. I will always remember how he told me he held me in his heart—close in his heart—and that he needed to tell me something.

I hate to admit this, but I felt that old, old stab of fear and panic, thinking he was going to break up with me and then leave. Why do I always fear the worst? I hate that about me. But I love the way Todd calms me and brings me back to a place of truth and hope every time. I started to cry, and he touched my face and said, "You need to know, Kilikina, that I love you." Whenever he calls me by my Hawaiian name, I melt, and I melted today when he told me he loved me. Then he told me a second time and said we have a couple of months to pray through what the future holds for us.

Hold this dearly precious secret for me, okay?

Todd said he loves me.

My heart is wearing a very big smile right now.

## July 4th
### (Happy Birthday, America!)

Silent Sis,

I miss America so much today. I miss my home, family, and friends. Most of all I miss Todd. No surprise there. When I made the decision to stay here for this final summer session, I thought it would go quickly. But after being with Todd and Katie for all those weeks, it has been so hard to get back into the studies and into spending time with the kids at the orphanage. I want to finish out my time here well. It's been an amazing, wonderful experience in many ways, and I'm glad I came. But I can't wait to go home. Ah, home. Even writing it makes me feel a little sad and lonely.

However, I'm determined not to get depressed or apathetic during my final weeks here. Todd told me right before he returned to California that, for each of the sixty-seven days I'm still here, we'll pretend it's one long day like he experienced at the Arctic Circle where the sun doesn't set in the summer. And every time we think about each other during this one long day, we'll say, "I can't wait until tomorrow."

So, I better say it quickly now before I start to think about fireworks, hot dogs, and watermelon. I can't wait until tomorrow.

## September 10

My Sweet Silent Sister,

I can't decide if I stepped out of a dream or into a dream. One of these places doesn't seem real. Was Switzerland real? I'm sure it was. But here I am at Rancho Corona University, rooming with Katie, seeing Todd every day, and it's like this is the only life I've ever known. So this must be the dream, right?

No, I guess it's all real. I have to say the best part is that everything here feels familiar. I got along fine with my roommates in Switzerland. But sharing a room with Katie is so much easier. She is definitely my Forever Friend.

I spent some time reading my Bible this morning and marked a verse in the first chapter of John: "Yet to all who received him, to those who believed in his name, he gave the right to become children of God."

I have been given the right to become one of God's children because I've received Him into my heart and life and I've believed in His name. It's like God has adopted me into His family.

This really gets to me because I keep thinking about all the children at the orphanage and how they were waiting for someone to adopt them. I guess the best thing I can do now that I can't hug them and be with them is to pray for them. I'm going to do that now.

## September 12

Ooo, SS, listen to this verse. It really got to me.

"Give freely without begrudging it, and the Lord your God will bless you in everything you do" (Deuteronomy 15:10).

I needed to read that today. Todd asked me to do some stuff to help him out, and I was gritting my teeth and doing it because I felt like I had to and not because I wanted to. Then I saw this verse in some of the material I'm studying for one of my classes. If I don't give willingly and joyfully, regardless of whether I'm giving my time or effort or even my love, then I'm not giving freely. And if I'm not giving freely, then is it even a gift? That last part really got to me. I mean, I want God to bless me. So why am I not willing to freely bless Todd? Or Katie? Or anyone else here on my floor in the dorm? It's too easy for me to close up and pull back and not want to give freely.

Hold this thought for me, will you? I need to think about it some more.

## September 16

Hey there, Silent Sister,

Did I tell you Matthew Kingsley is going to school here at Rancho? I don't think I did. It turns out that Katie knew him from their softball connection last semester. She tried to tell me this summer about a guy she called number fourteen, which is the number he had on his jersey.

It's kind of odd how once you have tender feelings for someone you kind of always do, even if you're not romantically interested in them. Does that make sense? Todd and I are together. I mean really, truly together, and everyone here knows it. So it's not like I'm thinking about what it would be like to go out with Matthew, but even so, in some corner of my little-girl, boy-crazy brain, when I see him on campus I take a blip-trip to the "land of if-only" and wonder how different my life might have been if I had stayed in Wisconsin and if my family hadn't moved to California.

Okay. Enough with the mind-messing stuff. The reality of my life right now is that I'm very happy. I'm right where I want to be, and I know God has His hand on me. Hey! That's a little poem, isn't it? I'm right where I want to be and I know God has His hand on me!

I'm sitting in the chapel here on upper campus as I write, and the sunlight is coming through the stained glass windows, making the space glow with the amber light coming through the glass that makes up the crown in the window. It's so beautiful here. So peaceful. The stained glass reminds me of places we visited in Europe. I love this little sacred space here at the top of a campus filled with noise, people, and activity.

I came here to read my Bible and pray, and although I read two more chapters in John and did pray some, I have to admit all I can thing about is finding Katie right now. This past year when I was in Basel I often wished I could talk to her, but we had to coordinate schedules for calls, and emails never come out the same as conversations. She's right here on campus now. Somewhere. I'm going to go find her.

## September 19

Silent Sister,

My aunt is one confused woman. That's all I'm going to say. Father God, please do something to get her attention and bring her to you. I don't want her to leave Uncle Bob.

Why, oh why did she have to confide in me and make me promise to keep her secrets? What is she thinking?

## November 2

Oh, my Silent Sister,

I know I haven't written anything here for a long time, but I've been going through the worst, worst, worst time ever. Todd was in a serious car accidcnt and was in the hospital. He's doing all right now. He had a lot of stitches from the glass they had to remove, especially from his hands. While he's recuperating he's staying at Bob and Marti's, and I was there with him up until yesterday.

I thought I was going to lose him.

I really did. My heart has been in knots. While he was in the hospital, I finally told him I love him. I'd been waiting for the right moment once I knew that I knew for sure that I loved him with the sort of forever love he must have felt in Switzerland when he said he loved me.

We went to the desert before the accident for a weekend trip with the youth group at the church where he's working. On Saturday we were out in a dune buggy, and I knew I was ready to tell him. Just as I said the words, he turned on the engine, and it drowned out my declaration. I thought it was funny. Typical, right? I finally make a decision about something, a very important decision, and he can't hear me over the dune buggy roar.

It didn't bother me, but then he was in this horrible accident right after we got back. Gus the Bus was totaled.

I was sitting by his hospital bed, holding his hand, and I told him over and over in a whisper, "Todd, I love you." Again, he couldn't hear me. He was too sedated.

Then finally, yesterday, when he felt well enough to go out on the beach, I cooked breakfast for him at the campfire ring just like I tried to do all those years ago when the seagulls came and stole the eggs and bacon. This time I made sure the seagulls stayed away. More importantly, I was able to tell him face-to-face, "Todd, I love you."

I sort of blurted it, but it didn't matter that the moment wasn't sweet, dainty, and romantic. I said it. I meant it. Todd heard me. He knows. He knew all along.

And oh, the kiss we shared after I told him! The bacon on the griddle over the flame was sending up fireworks. And a whole other set of fireworks were lighting up inside me.

I told him three times that I loved him, and yes, I cried. Of course I cried. You know how the tears just spill out of me. I mean, a few weeks ago I thought he might die. I really did. So to have him beside me and healing up the way he is got to me.

Todd said that when a thing is spoken three times it is established. I don't know exactly what that means to him, but to me it means I was certain. I'm not changing my mind.

It really was the most wonderfully perfect time we've had together in a long time. We laughed, kissed, prayed, ate, and teased each other. It was perfect. So perfect that something inside of me thought it would be the right time for him to propose.

I know. I'm always wanting more, aren't I? Never quite content. It's an old problem. I really wish I wouldn't let those insecure thoughts enter into my mind. They always bring their disruptive pals, doubt and fear. And when the three of them set up their den in my spirit, they create disaster every time.

Go away, insecurity. Be gone, doubt. Shove off, fear. You are NOT welcome here. My heart is a place created for love, joy, and peace. Jesus, guard my heart. Lead me in paths of righteousness for your name's sake. And thank you for saving Todd's life and for healing him. Please continue to do your good work in his life.

## November 10

Me again, Silent Sister.

So much has been happening in my heart and life. I talked to Donna, my manager at the campus bookstore where I work. She had some wise things to say, including the importance of writing things down.

Right now I can't imagine going on in my life without being partnered with Todd in whatever comes our way. It seems so natural and like such a perfect fit.

I know he's going to propose soon. I just know it. Maybe before this weekend is over I'll hear those words dancing from his lips. I wonder how he'll ask me. I'm sure it will be creative.

Or maybe not. Todd has a very practical side to him, as well. I wouldn't be surprised if he just turned to me over tacos and said, "So, do you want to get married?"

I don't know how he will ask me or when, but I know I'm ready—more than ready—to say yes.

Yes, yes, a thousand times yes. I will marry you, Todd Spencer, and I will spend the rest of my life loving you with all my heart.

And one more thing. Donna told me to write everything down in detail. So I have one more detail to add. I love being in love. I love the way I wake each morning, and as soon as I do, I thing about Todd and how I'm wildly, completely in love with him, and I smile.

I've been smiling all the time lately. Nothing gets me down. Last week Katie said I had that mysterious glow of love in my cheeks. She said it looked as if my eyes were always laughing about some secret and that even my posture was improved. That made me laugh. She said Todd's love for me had made me beautiful and that my love for him was healing him.

All I know is that love has enabled me to soar higher into the heavens and into my relationship with God than I ever have gone before. Love has given me breath, as I've plunged deeper into the ocean of understanding and patience. Love has focused my eyes to the minutest details, as minor as a ladybug inching across a daisy petal. At the same time, love has enlarged my embrace so I can gather friends and family closer to my heart than ever before.

Love is... oh, how I wish I had the words. Love is God's greatest gift and His most cherished reward. It is the echo of His own heart, sounded back to Him by us, His children, so that a decaying world might see firsthand the power of resurrection and new life. Love is all I know in my world right now.

I feel like laughing at my own giddiness.

I realize that I'm such a virgin in every way. I have never tasted a sensation as intoxicating as being in love. It has me reeling. Ha! I'm emotionally drunk on God's greatest gift, love. Imagine that!

## November 21

Hello, Silent Sister.

I got baptized tonight. I've been thinking about it for quite a while, and tonight seemed the right time to respond to the invitation at church. It was an important, sacred moment. When I came up out of the water, the pastor said, "Go in peace, for Christ Jesus, the Lord of your life, will be with you always."

And that's what I feel. His peace.

## November 24

Hi, Silent Sis.

This should be interesting. Todd and his dad are coming for Thanksgiving dinner at my parents' house. Uncle Bob and Aunt Marti are, too. Ever since Todd's accident, she seems to be re-entering her marriage. She didn't move to Santa Fe like she said she was going to. I don't know what she's been going through, but I've been praying for her.

## December 10

Silent Sis, are you ready for this!?

TODD PROPOSED!!!

Tonight! I still can't believe it! Well, I can believe it. Obviously I've been waiting for this, but the way he did it was pure Todd, all Todd. Oh, I'm so happy. So, so happy!

We all went to this new café and Christian bookstore called The Dove's Nest, and Rick was there. He's the manager! Crazy, huh? None of us knew. A whole group went, and the guys set up a joke on Katie as soon as they saw Rick, and he pulled it off flawlessly. But that's not what I want to write about. I mean, it was great fun and everything, but here's how Todd proposed.

Katie bought these candy hearts at Bargain Barn, her favorite place to shop. They were the sort of candy that has a short message on each piece. I don't know how old these were, but they had messages like "page me" and "sweet lips." We were going through them at the table, reading the messages, and Todd put one of the hearts in front of me that said, "Marry me." I didn't think anything of it.

Well, actually, I thought about when Katie urged me to make that Valentine's card for him with the same sort of candy hearts, and I had glued them to the card. Todd told me later that he peeled them off and ate them!

No one was eating the candy hearts at the table tonight. They were passing them around; so when Todd put a second candy heart in front of me that said, "Marry me," if you can believe this, I said, "I already have one of those." I was trying to make a sentence out of the phrases. I know, what a goof, right?

But then Todd put a third candy heart in front of me, and it also said, "Marry me." He lined all three of them up and said, "There. Once it's spoken three times, it's established. Forever."

I froze. I mean, inside I was freaking out. I knew this was it. He was really, truly, finally asking me to marry him!!!

Then he went down on one knee beside my chair, took my hands in his and said—oh! I get shivers just thinking of this— "Kilikina, my Kilikina, will you marry me?"

I immediately said, "Yes." It was barely a whisper. Then again I said, "yes" a little more loudly. Then to establish it, I said it a third time. "Yes! Todd, my Todd, I will marry you."

It was like the whole world stopped for just that fraction of a second. All I could hear was my heart beating, but I imagined it was my heart in rhythm with Todd's—two hearts beating as one.

The astounding thing was that all this happened between the two of us, and no one else seemed to notice. Katie asked Todd if he was on the ground because he had dropped one of the hearts. Then Katie looked at the line up of "Marry me" hearts in front of me, and she let out the biggest scream.

It was crazy after that. Hugs, cheers, kisses, and tears all around. All of our Forever Friends were there. Even Doug and Tracy. Oh, I will never forget this moment. Todd, oh, my Todd, you certainly surprised me. I didn't see it coming. Isn't it so like Todd to be spontaneous and yet in the spontaneity the truest feelings are all right on the surface and it feels so real? Right from the heart.

I LOVE TODD SPENCER, AND I AM GOING TO MARRY HIM!!!

# December 15

Christmas is in the air, Silent Sis!

My mom wanted to put a particular verse on our Christmas cards this year; so she asked me to look up the one about Jesus being the Prince of Peace. I found it for her. It's Isaiah 9:6 "For to us a child is born, to us a son is given, and the government will be on his shoulders. And he will be called Wonderful Counselor, Mighty God, Everlasting Father, Prince of Peace."

But when I was looking for that verse I found some other verses in Isaiah that I really liked. I knew I had to write them here because they definitely relate to what I've been feeling ever since Todd proposed. The verses are in Isaiah 43:11, 13, 18 and 19.

"I, even I, am the LORD, and apart from me there is no savior... Yes, and from ancient days I am he. No one can deliver out of my hand. When I act, who can reverse it?... Forget the former things; do not dwell on the past. See, I am doing a new thing! Now it springs up; do you not perceive it?"

To that question I wholeheartedly answer, "Yes, I do see it! I feel it spring up inside me every time Todd and I are together. Being engaged is a brand-new thing." I know this might be over-spiritualizing our engagement (not like Todd would ever do something like that—ha!), but I really feel as if God had this all planned out from long ago. Even through all the ups and downs that Todd and I went through, when it was the right time, it was like God put everything together for us.

Yesterday I was wishing I hadn't gone to Switzerland for so long because I missed that whole year of being with Todd. But we're together now, and I'm not going to dwell on the past. Why go back and get stuck in the land of "if only"? God is doing a new thing with us. This is the time for us to move forward together and enjoy every minute of it.

And yes, I do realize that my saying God had planned from long ago for Todd and me to end up together could launch a whole tangled theological discussion with some of my friends here at Rancho Corona. So I won't say it to them. I'll just say it to you, my wonderful Silent Sis. You are a pro at keeping my thoughts just between us.

That brings up a point. Hmmm. I hadn't thought of this before. Do you think I should ever let Todd read this? Would he be at all interested in what I've thought about ever since I first met him? Or do only women get into all this reflecting and processing on paper?

I'll have to think about whether I want him to read my diary. It's not like I have anything in here to hide from him. It's just weird to think about sharing any of this since for so long I've come here to process what I was thinking about him. Do I want him to know what I was thinking?

Okay. Enough reflecting. I need to run. Or as my fiancé has always said, "Later."

(Hee-hee! I just wrote fiancé with the little accent and everything! Why is it that I am just giddy over all these little happy bits that come with being engaged?)

## December 28

Well, Silent Sister,

I have learned so many interesting things about what happens once you become engaged. Here are a few of my observations:

1) You lose a significant number of brain cells so that you have to double-think every question on every exam, and you forget what you told people and where you put things.
2) Making a final decision on wedding basics such as your engagement ring becomes all-consuming.
3) Your immune system caves in. At least Todd's did, and he spent Christmas at our house with a beast of a cold. (And by the way, my throat is starting to hurt. I told Todd I wasn't going to get sick just because he did, and he grinned and said, "Yes, dear." I hate to say this, but I think he might be right. Oh, man, I don't have time to get sick!)

To continue the list of observations:

4) Your aunt decides when and where she thinks you should get married even after you and your fiancé already have decided on the meadow of upper campus at Rancho Corona and the beautiful date of May 22. You're just waiting for the right moment to tell everyone after you get the confirmation on the meadow.

5) Your roommate spends a suspicious amount of time being unusually comfortable around Rick Doyle.

6) The rest of the world keeps going at its standard pace without making allowances for all the adjustments you're dealing with. It's as if no one has ever been in love before and therefore doesn't realize how exhausting engagement bliss can be!

## January 9

Silent Sister, don't laugh.

Todd was right. I got the flu. And he was also right that it's a killer of a bug. I'm still in bed after four days of misery. At least I'm over the achy fever part and into the laryngitis phase.

This afternoon I pulled out the shoebox I've kept under my bed for at least five years now. I covered the box with wrapping paper years ago, and inside are fourteen letters sealed up in individual envelopes. The front of each envelope reads, "To my future husband." Every time I wrote one of those letters, I prayed for him, whoever he might be, and I wrote a short note telling him that I was saving myself for him and praying that God would lead and protect him.

I was thinking this would be a good time to write another letter, and I realized this is the first time I'll be writing one knowing the name of the man to put on the envelope. I know who my future husband will be.

Todd.

Just thinking about that fills me with such a sweet sense of hope and contentment. Todd. I have no voice right now to say his name aloud, but I can write it all out. I bought some beautiful stationery in Switzerland, and I'm going to use that to write this next letter.

What should I say? I think I'll practice here and then copy it on the stationery.

Dear Future Husband, my Todd,

As I write this, you're in Mexico, and I'm in bed with the flu. I've had some time to think these past few days, and I want to tell you two things. No, three.

First, I'm so happy we're getting married. I can't wait to be your wife. I know we'll have a lot of adjusting to do, but we'll work on it together. I know we'll become better communicators.

And that brings me to my second thought. Whenever I'm sick, I need attention. I don't like to be left alone to sweat it out.

I'd like you to check on me and bring me tea and toast. I know we're different in this area, and I thought you should know this is important to me.

I remember one time in high school when I was sick, and you came to my parents' house and sat by my bed doing your homework while I slept. Maybe you thought that once I woke up I'd spring out of bed, and we could go do something. But you were there with me. I never told you that I considered that one of the most romantic and tender memories of our early years together. I can't wait until we're married so that every morning when I wake up the first thing I'll see is your handsome face. Soon.

Now, on to my final thought before I get lost in a daydream about our future together. I want all our children to have middle names, okay?

> With all my love, forever,
> Your Christina Juliet Miller
> (soon to be Spencer)!
> P.S. I love you.

## January 9

Yes, it's me again, SS.

And yes, it's the same day. I wanted to mark the moment I had with my mom today. After I wrote my letter to Todd, Mom came in my room, and we ended up talking about wedding dresses. She pulled her wedding dress out of a box in her closet, and I tried it on. It needs a lot of adjusting, but I decided I want to use the top part of her dress, have it altered, and then have her make a different skirt for it. She loved the idea. She was so touched.

I really want to do this. I'm not just trying to make her happy. This is something that will make me happy. We had the best talk. It was like talking to a close friend. My mom and I have never really been like that.

She was so cute when I sat on her bed and she talked to me in hushed words about the sanctity of being with your husband for the first time on your wedding night. Her words were very general and delicate, but I appreciated her talking about some of these things at last. It also made me think of how important it is for me to know that one day I'll sit on the edge of my bed with my daughter and tell her that her dad and I waited for each other and it was worth the wait. I want to have a story of hushed beauty when it comes to purity, just like my mom.

## February 4

Silent Sister,

My mother called this morning at 6:30. My grandpa, her father, passed away. We're all going to the funeral in Wisconsin. We leave Friday. I don't know what else to say.

## February 12

Hello, Silent Sis.

I'm not sure where to begin. My grandfather's funeral was touching in many ways. It was so good to see my grandma. She said she would come for the wedding. I really hope she does.

On the plane on the way home Todd gave me my engagement ring. We had it specially designed, and it took a long time to get it. I didn't know Todd had it. He said he was planning on giving it to me at the beach on Saturday, which is where we're planning to go for Valentine's Day. But he said he couldn't wait, and he pulled it out and asked me all over again to marry him. I said yes all over again. We kissed, and it was the best long, slow, promise-sealing kiss ever.

Oh, my heart! I am so in love with him it's ridiculous!

When we went to church the next day, Todd told the youth group about how he gave me the ring on the plane and how my face lit up.

Then Todd made the most incredible analogy between us being engaged and the way God views us. In the Bible God describes the church as the Bride of Christ. Todd said the Holy Spirit is like the engagement ring that God gives us as evidence of His promise that He will always love us and one day will come and take us to be His bride to live with Him forever.

It was amazing the way the students responded. Todd said that weddings on earth are a reflection of the great wedding feast of the Lamb that will happen when the Lord comes to take His bride, the Church, to be with Him.

I realized more deeply what a mystery that is. I felt so different and so much more in love with Todd after he placed the ring on my finger. I find myself growing more deeply in love with Christ as I see these parallels acted out in my life. Christ wants me and is waiting for me one day to be with Him forever. Until that day, His Holy Spirit in my life is evidence to others that I am promised to Him and I am waiting for Him.

That verse in Ephesians 4:30 makes more sense to me than it ever did before. "Do not grieve the Holy Spirit of God, with whom you were sealed for the day of redemption." Todd told the class it would be like my covering my ring finger with duct tape because I didn't want anyone to know I was engaged. He said that as my fiancé, it would break his heart if I did that. Yet we do the same thing when we don't let the Holy Spirit work in our lives.

Todd's charge to the class was to boldly let the whole world know that we're spoken for, that we belong to Christ. Then he said, "But if you're really in love with the Bridegroom, people will know instantly when they look at your face. Just look at Christy."

The whole group turned to stare at me, but I didn't care. My face and my whole heart were so brightly lit on fire with my love for God and Todd that I didn't feel at all embarrassed. I felt as if I were floating on clouds.

## February 12

One last thought, SS,

Todd was right about what he said to the teens. And Grandma was right, too, when I asked her for marriage advice and she told me, "It goes fast. It's over too soon. Keep short lists, honey. Learn to forgive quickly and go on because one day you'll wake up and find that somehow you grew old when you weren't looking. Your lists won't matter at all then."

What we're doing here isn't about this life only. The real us, our souls, will last forever. God wants us to say yes to His Son so we can be with Him forever. It's the ultimate "I do." The eternal "I promise."

Okay. I just had to get that down on paper. I am so fried. I have no idea how I'm going to manage to catch up with everything I have to do for school. This final semester is turning out to be much harder than I thought it would be. If you don't hear from me, it's only because I'm going to have to run very hard and very fast to pass all my classes and to actually graduate in May.

Can you believe I just said that? Graduate from college. Me. In only three months. I can't believe it.

## April 7

My Silent Sister,

I have one word: details! There are too many of these in my life. I'm never going to finish everything I need to do for my classes. I am never going to get everything finished in time for the wedding. Why, oh, why did we decide on May 22? Why didn't we push the date out to August? I just want to be done with school right now! My brain can't hold another detail about anything!

## April 8

Isn't this perfect, Silent Sister?

Just the right verse, just when I needed it:

"Now all glory to God, who is able, through his mighty power at work within us, to accomplish infinitely more than we might ask or think" (Ephesians 3:20).

If I finish this semester, it's definitely going to be because of God's mighty power at work within me.

One of my professors has a sign on his desk that reads, "He who first taught us to trust in His name, has not thus far brought us to bring us to shame." I've read it so many times I have it memorized. I keep repeating it when I think I'm not going to accomplish all that I need to get done. God is in this. He's with me. He's leading me. He can do even more thank I ask of Him.

Thank You, Lord. Thank You, thank You for being with me every step of the way.

Now, back to studying I go.

## April 30

Silent Sis,

Sweet news! Or I should say, awesome news! Doug and Tracy are going to have a baby—did I tell you that? I don't remember. The awesome news is that they found out it's going to be a boy. They want to name him Daniel. I'm so happy for them!

I can't imagine what it would be like to be preggers and walk around with a big belly like Tracy. She looks pretty cute, but she also looks pretty uncomfortable when she tries to bend over.

One day. I hope. Todd is going to be a great dad. But first he's going to be a great husband. And before that happens, I have a whole lot of things to finish!

Ta-ta for now!

# May 15

Oh, Silent Sister, can you believe it?

One week from today I will be a married woman. I can't believe it. Katie helped me to move my things into our apartment, and I realized how pathetically poor we are.

Here's the inventory of our worldly possessions:

1) A custom, one-of-a-kind surfin' sofa that Todd made using the back rest of a salvaged benchseat from ole' Gus the Bus and his beloved surfboard "Naranja," which serves as the nice bright orange seat. That's all I'm going to say about it at this point, except I have a feeling it will be with us for a long time; so Katie and I gave it a name: "Narangus."

2) A nice new bed that Todd's dad bought for us. I do have to say that I worried just a little that Todd would want us to have a bed like the one he had at that apartment he shared with Doug and Rick in San Diego. It was just a big box with sand. Aaaaa, no.

3) Todd's old dresser.

4) The bookshelf Todd and I bought all those years ago at a garage sale. It could use some fresh paint. The dusty rose is really dusty now.

5) One potted daisy and a welcome mat at the front door,

thanks to Katie and her heroic effort to help me perk up the place.

6) Three paper cups, one coffee mug, a stack of paper plates, a box of tissues, hand soap and hand lotion by the kitchen sink and six chocolate chip cookies from the bakery, again, thanks to Katie.

7) One poster of a waterfall highlighting the bridge Todd jumped off of in Maui.

8) Oh, and my faithful Winnie the Pooh that Todd bought for me at Disneyland eons ago.

9) One patchwork blanket my grandmother made for me when I was in elementary school.

There. Isn't that the inventory every young married couple needs to set up house?

## May 21

Sweetie Pie, oh, Silent Sis,

TOMORROW!!!

Today is the last day that I will be Christina Juliet Miller. Tomorrow at this time I will become Christina Juliet Spencer. Eeeeeee!

I have my letters to my future husband all ready to take on our honeymoon. I ended up taking them out of the individual envelopes and folding them up all nice and neat into a little bundle. Then I tied them with some lace ribbon my mom had in with her sewing things.

I can't wait to give them to Todd. I hope he doesn't think they're silly. He won't. Will he? It doesn't matter. I'm going to give them to him, and he can say whatever he wants.

We're going to Maui for our honeymoon. Did I tell you that? Thanks to Uncle Bob, of course. We're staying at Uncle Bob's condo. It's the same one we went to for my sixteenth birthday. Never did I guess then that I'd be returning for our honeymoon!

Oh! I just realized that one of the letters I wrote to my future husband, aka TODD, was written at that same condo. Is that amazing or what? Full circle, right? Wow. I do feel like the most spoiled bride ever. No, not spoiled. I take that back. I am blessed. So blessed.

I've been thinking a lot about what it's going to be like being with Todd completely for the first time. You know what I mean. And I've come to the conclusion that he and I will just have to figure out how we fit together as we go along. It will be the first time for him and the first time for me, and together we'll just figure it out. I am so, so, so excited! (And a tiny bit nervous.) But mostly I'm excited and happy, and I just can't believe this day is finally here!

TOMORROW!!!

Oh, and by the way, I managed to finish everything that I needed to do in all my classes, I graduated, and all the details for the wedding have been completed. So why did I spend so much time worrying? I don't even think it's dawned on me that I'm now a college graduate.

I have a job, too. That was another God-thing. I'm working at the bookstore next to the Dove's Nest Café where Katie works. How amazing is that? When I get back from the honeymoon, I'll work in the same building every day with Katie.

I mean it: I am blessed. God has blessed me in more ways than I have even stopped to count.

TOMORROW!!!

## May 31

Hi, hi, Silent Sis.

I hope you understand why I didn't take you along on our honeymoon. We're back now and, oh wow! I mean, WOW! Todd and I are definitely "Happily Mauied." Our wedding was amazing, beautiful, and perfect. It's still like a dream. The happiest of all dreams. And our honeymoon was really, really, really wonderful.

I know you're probably wondering about how it was for us when we were finally able to give ourselves to each other, or as Todd said, quoting Genesis (of course he has a Bible verse for everything!), we could be "naked and not ashamed." And we were. I mean, it was a little oddish and embarrassing right at first, but that's because everything was new and unfamiliar territory. But it was so natural and beautiful. It really is an amazing way to express our love for each other. I can see why God made this full expression something to be shared only between one man and one woman for the rest of their lives. It's so intimate. Not like in the movies.

Katie was asking me what it was like, and I realized that even thinking about Todd and me being together completely, mind, body and soul, was intimate. Just between Todd and me. It wasn't something for me to report even to my best friend. Again, it wasn't like in the movies.

She honored my privacy and discretion, but she said she wanted me to tell her that the purity part of it isn't a hoax. She said she needed to know that what she was saving for her future husband would be worth the wait.

I told her, "Oh, it's worth the wait, all right. Definitely." I told her to trust me, and she said something about how happy I looked and how my face was glowing. I also told her that she would be glad she saved those hundreds of kisses she wanted to give away to different guys over the years. I told her that, once she got on the other side of the longing and was a married woman, she would be free to break open the bank. After I said that much, I just couldn't finish the sentence. I didn't know how to express it. I said something like, "You'll have to finish that sentence for yourself one day."

I know that wasn't a very good answer, and I'm sure it wasn't what she was hoping to hear.

All I will tell you, dear Silent Sis, is that I'm a very happily married woman. Not that everything is perfect between us, but we have our lives ahead of us to figure out what works and doesn't work. And that should be half the fun, right?

## June 29

It's Baby Daniel Day, Silent Sis!

We went to the hospital to see Doug, Tracy, and baby Daniel. He is SO cute! I got to hold him and kiss his bald little head. He was 7 pounds and 14 ounces. My baby-clueless husband thought Daniel was 14 pounds and 7 ounces! If he was, ouch! Poor Tracy.

Doug had to tell all of us that he cut the umbilical cord. Katie stopped him before he said any more. Thank you, Katie. I'm sure I'll want to know a lot more baby details when it's our turn some day, but for now I'd rather not hear those sorts of particulars.

My favorite moment of the visit was right when we were leaving and I had to give baby Daniel back to Tracy. Todd went over to the bed, placed his hand on Daniel's little head, and blessed him. It was the most solemn, striking moment for all of us. Katie, Tracy, and I all got teared up and exchanged this beautiful, womanly smile. I can't believe we're all grown up and sharing these huge life experiences.

Daniel really is adorable. I loved holding him. I wish we didn't live so far away from them. It takes about an hour to get to Carlsbad, which isn't bad, but then it's an hour home, and that's always the killer.

## July 13

Silent Sister, hi, hi, hi.

Oh, I do love being married! Todd and I had the most romantic dinner last night. I made chicken, baked potatoes, and green beans that I bought on the way home from a roadside stand. Then we had watermelon for dessert. I'm not saying I'm a great cook or anything. The chicken was pretty dry, actually. But I splurged and bought real butter for the potatoes, and the green beans were fresh and tasted just right.

We ate slowly and talked, laughed, and kissed a bunch of times in between bites. The whole dinner our feet were cozied up under our little kitchen table. I know that sounds strange—like we were holding feet instead of holding hands, but that is kind of what it was like.

After we ate, we kept leaning across the table, kissing and whispering and kissing some more. Then we did what married people get to do with sweet abandon.

When I woke up this morning, I turned and looked at my husband. He was awake and just lying there, staring at me. I told him that being married to him is so much better and more amazing than I ever dreamed it would be. Todd said I was beautiful. He said it over and over. It's like all the things I wished he would say to me over the years while we were dating he's saying to me now. And they mean so much because we're "us." We're together. We're married. I believe him when he tells me he loves me and that I'm beautiful.

This might seem like a funny jump from that thought, but at work today I was thinking about all this, and I saw Katie talking to Rick, smiling at him and him smiling back at her. They're pretty much together now. She says it's not really official. But I was trying to find a way to tell her to be careful and not to give her heart away to Rick completely. I know the reason I feel that way is because back in high school he was such a smooth talker, and I found myself going along with him just because I liked the way he made me feel.

At the time, I really wanted Todd to be the one to say all the sweet things to me and tell me that I looked good, but he didn't. Now that Todd is free to give me all these compliments, they mean so much more than the surface kind of flirty things Rick used to say to me.

I just hope Katie isn't letting Rick feed that insecure part of her that's longing for attention and affirmation. I'm trying to be supportive of their relationship. Rick has changed A LOT.

Everyone has seen that. Still, I have a sisterly sort of concern for Katie.

I'm glad she's going to be an RA this year at Rancho Corona. It's her senior year, and I think she's going to be great in that position. Plus I think it will give her something to do so she won't become too wrapped up in Rick.

## August 16

Fun times, SS!

Todd is having some great times with the kids in the youth group this summer. It's his job, but I know he'd be doing all this even if it wasn't. He's really good with them, and more teens come every week.

Tonight he taught from the book of 1 John and said all these great things about love—God's love and human love. All the girls kept looking at me to see if I agreed with what he said. I'm sure they could tell by my continual smile that I'm Todd's biggest supporter, and I totally agreed with what he said.

I wanted to be sure to write down the verses I liked the most from his talk. I want to memorize these verses. They're out of 1 John 4.

"God is love. When we take up permanent residence in a life of love, we live in God and God lives in us... There is no room in love for fear. Well-formed love banishes fear.

Since fear is crippling, a fearful life—fear of death, fear of judgment—is one not yet fully formed in love.

"We, though, are going to love—love and be loved. First we were loved, now we love. He loved us first."

It's so true. God loved us first. He keeps pouring out His love on us and teaching us how to love others the way He loves. And His perfect love casts out all fear. That's how it says it in the translation of the Bible that I have.

I think about how afraid I was of so many things for a long time. I look back on the things I worried about with Todd and how I was afraid I'd never see him again when he left for Hawai'i and then for Spain.

I know this isn't exactly what those verses are talking about in 1 John, but in a lot of ways it applies to how things were inside of me. My love wasn't fully formed yet. Neither my love for God nor for Todd. And I know they aren't fully mature yet. But Todd and I are so much further along than we were five years ago or even five months ago. Our love for each other keeps growing and as it does, I find I don't have any of those old fears. They're gone. For me it's becoming the same way with God. The more I'm growing in my love for Him, the more I know Him and trust Him. I feel God's love for me more now, and it's growing stronger the longer I'm a Christian. It really is a relationship because it keeps growing and changing.

Father God, You have been so good to me. Thank You for loving me. I want to love You more.

## September 6

Hello, Silent Sister.

My husband is driving me crazy! Can I just say that here and you won't tell anyone how frustrated I am at the moment?

It's a stupid thing, really. We had this argument about how he leaves his bath towel on the floor after he uses it. He expects me to pick it up and put it in the laundry, and then when it's all nice, fresh, clean, and dry, I'm supposed to hang it on the towel rack.

Where did he get that idea? Why can't he hang it on the towel rack or put it in the dirty clothes basket himself? Why is it that every time I use the bathroom, I have to trip over one of his wadded up towels?

I tried to talk to him about this before he left this morning, and he said I was too "hormonal." WHAT!? Since when did he start telling me I was being "hormonal"?

I'm so mad at him!

And I'm mad at myself, too, because I know later, when I think about this, my response is going to seem petty and ridiculous. The towel part, that is. Not the part about his saying I'm hormonal. That has to be the worst word in the whole English language. Is it even in the dictionary? I'm going to look it up.

But first I seriously need some chocolate. I hope we have some brownies left. Oh, yeah. So, I made them last night when I got home from work, and Todd started to devour them before we even had dinner. He kept saying thank you for making them, as if no one ever made brownies for him before.

I guess no one ever has.

That doesn't mean I'm not still mad at him about his incurable towel habit and the insensitive comment.

Katie once said that Todd was "detail impaired." She was right. I think she described him that way when he had the shopping list for the youth group trip and I put down "two dozen wire coat hangers." He decided to buy two plastic coat hangers instead. Needless to say, no one could roast marshmallows that night at the campfire with only two plastic coat hangers!

Marshmallows sound good right now. I wonder if we have any?

## October 21

Hey there, Silent Sister.

The Katie-and-Rick saga is getting interesting. Rick's roommate, Eli, was over the other night, and he was talking to Todd and me about Katie—what a great personality she has and how he doesn't think Rick realizes what a great person she is.

Eli and Todd met each other back when Todd was in Spain, and Todd worked it out so that Eli could share Rick's apartment now. They just live a few doors down from us, which is bizarre, but not really because this is a small town and this is the nicest apartment complex for the lowest rent.

Anyway, I told Todd after Eli left that I was pretty sure Eli has a crush on Katie. Todd gave me one of those half-grins like even if he knew something on that topic he wouldn't be able to tell me because he would be betraying a trust.

The thing is, Katie and Rick are getting really serious about each other. At least I think they are. She and I haven't had a heart-to-heart in quite awhile. It's time for us to go to lunch.

It's funny. Katie calls Eli "Goatee Guy." That's what she dubbed him at our wedding.

Which reminds me. I never wrote down something that happened at our wedding that I don't want to forget. Rick and Doug thought it would be clever to do some rearranging with our honeymoon luggage to make room for their "honeymoon survival kit." They took out my stack of letters that I had all ready to give to Todd with the lace ribbon tied around them and everything.

Katie found out, and she came dashing after our limo as we were leaving the reception. She screamed at the driver until he stopped, and then she tumbled into the limo and tried to discretely give me the letters so Todd wouldn't know what was going on.

Believe me, I was so grateful! And so mad at Doug and Rick for being boys, I guess. They didn't know what the letters were. Katie knew. Wonderful Katie. Where would I be without my favorite "Peculiar Treasure"?

She asked me when we got back from our honeymoon if I ever gave the letters to Todd, and I did. I gave them to him our second night on Maui. After we had dinner that night, he read them by candlelight on the front deck, or lanai, as they call it. The ocean stretched out before us, and in the distance was the island of Molokai with a few scattered lights along the shore.

When Todd and I were at Uncle Bob's condo on my sixteenth birthday, he and I sat in the same place and talked about our relationship, such as it was at that point. Todd said it was like the lights on Molokai that were so far away that we couldn't make out what they were. Todd said we needed just to keep moving forward in our relationship, toward the light, so to speak. He said the closer we got the clearer it would become, and we'd know what we should do.

And there we were, on our honeymoon, on the same deck, looking out across the ocean at the same lights, and Todd was reading all the letters I'd written to him over the years. It was a perfect moment. Perfect.

Todd cried. I cried.

I'm so glad I wrote those letters. I'm so glad Katie ran after the limo. I'm so glad Todd didn't laugh at the letters or at me. He does that sometimes. He laughs at things I say or do, and it bugs me so much because I'm not trying to be funny. But that's Todd. That is totally Todd. It always has been. I love that man. And I'm pretty sure I will always love him. Forever. Sigh.

## April 2

I found you, Silent Sister!

I have no idea how you ended up on the floor, behind the bed's headboard. I seriously thought you had been stolen. Do you know how many times I searched for you? That's one of the disadvantages of your being a "Silent" Sister. You never called out from behind the headboard to tell me where you had gotten stuck.

I'm glad you're back. No worse for the hiding, I hope. But you are running out of pages. What am I going to do when you fill up, too, the way my Dear Silent Friend filled up? Maybe I'll have to go back to Italy to buy a twin sister where I bought you.

Wouldn't that be nice? Man, that seems so long ago. Like another lifetime. So much has changed.

I just sat here and read everything I wrote in this extended journal, and I'm amazed. Stunned, really, at all that I've recorded over the years. So much has happened.

One thing that I realized, as I was reading, is that God has been so good to me all the way through. I can see His leading in the way a lot of things have happened in my life. There are so many God-things. I know that when I wrote a lot of the diary entries, I couldn't see God's hand at all. But now that I look back, I can see where He was protecting me or directing me, but I didn't realize what was going on.

I heard someone at work the other day say, "Make sure you do it with love. Only what is done in love will last."

I've been thinking about that. Love, God's love, endures. It covers a multitude of sins. That's a verse isn't it? I just looked it up. It is. First Peter 4:8, "Most important of all, continue to show deep love for each other, for love covers a multitude of sins."

A year ago right now I was panicked about preparing everything for the wedding while trying to finish college. I can't believe it was a year ago. Now it feels as if Todd and I have been married forever. Well, maybe not forever, but for much longer than eleven months.

In some ways both of us have had to grow up a lot. We've had to figure out a bunch of stuff like our finances. Every month there's enough to pay all our bills, and that's definitely a miracle. It never seems as if we're going to have enough, but we always do.

Todd is adamant about giving back to God off the top from both our paychecks. And not just the ten percent tithe like it talks about in the Bible. He says that as a family we're going to always give a tithe and offerings. So we give generously, and somehow, (God, I'm sure) there's enough every month. I knew living with Todd would stretch my faith, and it has.

The other thing about marriage that I didn't expect is how long it takes us to talk things through sometimes. I can't believe how many minor arguments we've had and how long it takes to resolve them. We're getting better at it, though. We're getting better at arguing, at expressing ourselves, and at loving each other more. I guess in some ways it feels as if we just met a few weeks ago because we both keep saying, "I didn't know that about you."

Strange. How can it feel as if we've been married for twenty years, and at the same time feel as if we just met? I don't know. But it does. I love Todd. I love being married to Todd. (Even if he STILL leaves his wet bath towel on the floor.

Sometimes. Not all the time now. About twenty percent of the time. And I still don't remember to close the kitchen cupboards all the way, which drives Todd crazy. But I'm getting better.)

Katie said that Todd and I are knit together at the heart. I think we are.

Now, as far as Katie being knit together at the heart with Rick… not happening. She's going to graduate in a few weeks. I'm really hoping she'll get some clarity as to what to do next. I guess instead of hoping I need to pray more for her.

## April 28

Hello Dear Silent Sister,

Todd's position at the church where he works has been a bit unstable. I'm trying not to be nervous that he'll be laid off or at least have his hours cut. I know that God always works these things out. Who was it that said worry was like a rocking chair? It keeps you busy, but you don't get anywhere.

## May 19

Hello, my Silent Sister.

So it looks as if Katie will move in with us. Just for a little while until her apartment is ready. And what apartment is that, you may ask? Why, it's the same apartment that Rick and Eli

shared and are both moving out of. Katie will be just a f
doors down. I'd be more excited about that, I think, if thing
were more stable for us and if Katie had any idea at all wha
she's going to do for a job.

Our one-year anniversary is in a few days. I really had
hoped that Todd and I could do something extra fun like take
the day off and go to the beach, just the two of us. It's not looking very promising. I've thought about it a lot and decided not
to get my hopes up. If it doesn't work out, we can still have a
really nice time celebrating here. I'll make a big dinner for us
and light candles and make it extra special. We don't have to go
away. We just have to be together.

I'm going to have to ask Katie to find someone to hang out
with that night, but I need to do it in a nice way because she's
been acting pretty "hormonal" lately. And yes, I can't believe
I just wrote that about Katie because I can't stand it whenever
Todd has said that about me. (He doesn't say it anymore. I
let my feelings be known on that one awhile ago, and I think
he heard me.) But seriously, Katie has been bouncing all over
the place.

Her graduation last week was extra special because both
her parents came. I didn't think they would so I persuaded Uncle Bob and Aunt Marti to come as well as Doug and Tracy.
They had Danny Boy with them, and oh, is he a cutie! He's
a really active little baby. He wants to see what's going on all
the time.

It was good to see Doug and Tracy and get a chance to atch up. We promised each other we would connect again next month. Everyone is so busy all the time now.

It makes it nearly impossible to find a time when everyone can get together. But we'll figure it out. We have to. I don't want to be out of touch with our Forever Friends. We've spent too many years together to drift away from each other.

After Katie's graduation ceremony last week, Todd and I drove her to a celebration at Rick's parents' house, and I gave her my present in the car. She said she really liked it.

I didn't tell her how long it took me to put it together. It was a scrapbook. I searched for as many old photos of the two of us as I could find. Then I had them scanned and copied, and I put them in the album. I think she really likes it. I hope she does.

She was in a wedding today and got this crazy idea to hide a dove in her bouquet and then release it at the end of the ceremony.

She went to Escondido and saw my old boss, Jon, at the pet store. I was so bummed when she told me because I would have liked to go with her to see Jon. I can't believe he still works there.

I'll be eager to hear how her fine-feathered scheme turned out. Todd has a big meeting at church tonight to find out if he's going to be full-time during the summer.

# May 22

Sing with me, Sweet Silent Sis! Happy anniversary to us!

Can you believe it's been a year that Todd and I have been married? And can you believe it's been two years since I found you in the cute shop in Rome and brought you along for our splendid European adventure? You have been the best of bests.

And speaking of bests, not last night but the night before— sounds like a rhyme we used to chant when I would jump rope with Paula when we were kids—we had a crazy night.

First of all, the day before that, Katie moved in with us, and Todd found out the church was going to continue his contract for full-time through the summer. Eli moved out of his apartment. Rick moved to Redlands—I think it was Redlands. He's opening another restaurant, and he needed to be closer.

So two nights ago Katie was here, feeling very low, and I was trying to cheer her up when Todd came home. He'd been helping Eli move some of his furniture.

Katie was beyond bummed that Eli was leaving for Kenya in the morning. It was like she just discovered him after being on campus with him all school year and not really taking his interest in her seriously. I told her she should call him and tell im good-bye. Then, I don't know if it was Todd or me, but one of us reminded her of how she always wanted to go to Africa. I don't know what happened, but something seemed to break open inside her.

Within a few hours she packed up everything related to her life here and resolved to go to Kenya. We drove her to the airport, and she and Eli connected, and they boarded a plane. I guess. We haven't heard from her so I don't know exactly how everything turned out.

When Todd and I were driving home at six in the morning, we kept saying to each other, "That was a God-thing, right? It wasn't too random, was it? We didn't push her into anything, did we?"

I don't think we did. With someone else, possibly we could have pressed too much. But this is Katie. Independent, spontaneous Katie. Somehow it all seemed to fit.

So now we don't have Katie living with us, nor will she be moving into the apartment down the way.

Todd said this morning that, if I didn't mind, he'd like to spend our anniversary here in our apartment, just the two of us. Nice and quiet.

I got off work at the bookstore a little early and went to the grocery store. Oh, and how did I get to the store, you may ask? In my new car. Katie sold me her car for $1. As she was getting everything in order to go to Kenya, she asked if I had a dollar.

Then she gave me the pink slip for Clover. (That's what sr
named her car.) I didn't realize at the time what a huge blessing
this is. I have my own car! I've never had my own car. Katie is
the most amazing friend.

Anyway, I went to the grocery store to get what I needed
to make a nice anniversary dinner. Todd really likes this chick-
en I make that's coated with bread crumbs. I found a way to
make it so it doesn't get dried out. My mom told me to brush
the chicken with mayonnaise and then squirt lemon juice on
it before rolling it in the breadcrumbs. I'm not saying it's the
most health-conscious recipe, but Todd loves it. So I'm making Todd's Chicken, as we now call it, and baked potatoes and
green beans. He's going to be so happy. I even found some
coconut mango ice cream, which I know he's going to love.

Todd's Chicken is in the oven, I'm all freshened up, and I
set the table and lit candles. I love being married. Hurry home,
Todd! I'm ready to celebrate! Happy first anniversary to us!

## May 23

Quick note, Silent Sister.

Guess what I have sitting on our bedroom dresser right
now, filling the room with their spicy-sweet fragrance? That's
right. A dozen white carnations! Todd walked in the door last
night and had his hand behind his back. He had that little boy
grin of his, and his dimple was showing. Then he pulled out the

arnations, and he kissed me. It was just like the very first time he kissed me in the middle of the intersection when I was fifteen! Well, maybe not exactly like that time because that time Bob and Marti were waiting for me in the car and the light turned green and people were honking at us.

But what was the same was the way that he looked at me right before he kissed me. It was the same look he gave me before our very first kiss, as if our standing there face-to-face was the most amazing and important moment and one that he didn't want to miss for the world. It was so sweet and so rich. His look and his kiss were full of love.

I'm telling you, I could fall in love with this guy all over again.

Now, I have to face reality, don't I? I have to admit that I've come to the last of your lovely, blank pages, dear Silent Sister. Thank you for giving your empty self to me and allowing me to place my many scattered thoughts here for safe keeping. You know I'll keep you for always. I'll visit you many times before my life is over. And hopefully, I won't lose you again for months at a time!

I know that you will continue to make me laugh aloud. You'll probably catch a few more of my salty tears when I read the words that you and my Dear Silent Friend have both graciously held for me all these years.

Perhaps one day you'll see an unfamiliar pair of eyes scan-

ning your pages, and you'll feel a different pair of hands ho
ing you. Those eyes and those hands will quite possibly belor.
to my daughter. (And no, I'm not trying to drop a surprise or.
you here. Todd and I aren't expecting a baby. But I hope we
will someday.)

And if we do have a daughter and if she grows up and
wants to know what I was like when I was her age, I will invite
her to read the words you've so patiently held for me because
I'll want her to know that what she's feeling is normal. And I'll
want her to know that her mother was a goof sometimes. And
was overly emotional sometimes. But more than anything, I'll
want her to see the ways that God worked in her mother's and
father's lives. These entries will give evidence that we were a
couple of a God Lovers who were extremely blessed.

And she will also know that even before she was con-
ceived, she already was tucked away in a special corner in the
secret place in my heart.

Forever,
Christina Juliet Miller Spencer
(Kilikina)

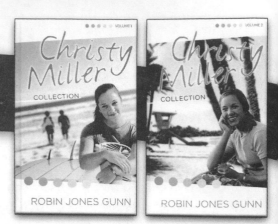

# The Friendships Continue

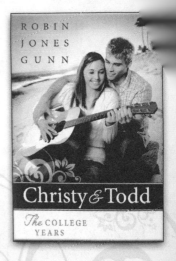

Christy & Todd The College Years

Sierra Jensen Collection, Volume 1 (Books 1-3)

Sierra Jensen Collection, Volume 2 (Books 4-6)

Sierra Jensen Collection, Volume 3 (Books 7-9)

Sierra Jensen Collection, Volume 4 (Books 10-12)

# List of Books by Robin Jones Gunn

Robin Jones Gunn is the author of more than 70 books including:

The Christy Miller Series
Christy Miller Volume 1, 2, 3, 4

The Sierra Jensen Series
Sierra Jensen Volume 1, 2, 3, 4

Christy & Todd: The College Years

The Katie Weldon Series
Peculiar Treasures
On a Whim
Coming Attractions

Forever Friends: A Journal

The Glenbrooke Series
Secrets
Whispers
Echoes
Sunsets
Clouds
Waterfalls
Woodlands
Wildflowers

The Sisterchicks® Series

Gardenias for Breakfast
Under a Maui Moon

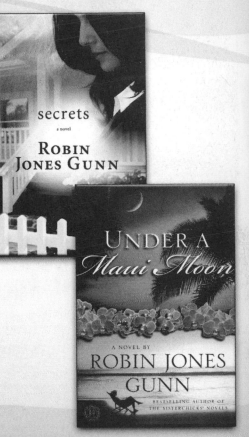

To purchase Robin's books and fun gift items, visit her online shop at
shop.robingunn.com

# Connect With Robin

Facebook – robingunn.com/facebook
Twitter – robingunn.com/twitter
Robin's Nest Newsletter Sign up at
robingunn.com

# Robin's Online Shop

Forever ID Bracelets
T-Shirts
Key Chains
Posters
Books
Visit Robin's Online Shop at
shop.robingunn.com